"Look, Mr. Archer..."

"Dillon," he said softly.

"I have to get along with you," Heidi said. "I don't have to like you."

"That's all right. Liking isn't precisely the word I had in mind." Dillon drew a casual finger down the side of Heidi's face, tracing the hairline from brow to ear. She couldn't quite suppress a shiver.

"What do you call that, Heidi?"

"How about loathing?"

Dillon smiled. "No," he said softly. "Oh, no...."

Leigh Michaels has been a writer since she was old enough to figure out how to hold a pencil, but publishing a romance novel was an ambition she kept secret from everyone except her husband— her biggest supporter. They mailed her first manuscript together on Friday the 13th, which she says has been her lucky day ever since.

She finds writing to be like tiptoeing into a parallel universe that's always waiting just around the corner from real life. All the people from her books live there and sometimes interact in unexpected ways, making going to work every day a new adventure.

Leigh loves to hear from readers; you can write to her at P.O. Box 935, Ottumwa, IA 52501-0935.

Books by Leigh Michaels

INVITATION
TO LOVE
Leigh Michaels

Harlequin Books

TORONTO • NEW YORK • LONDON
AMSTERDAM • PARIS • SYDNEY • HAMBURG
STOCKHOLM • ATHENS • TOKYO • MILAN
MADRID • WARSAW • BUDAPEST • AUCKLAND

ISBN 0-373-03352-4

INVITATION TO LOVE

Copyright © 1994 by Leigh Michaels.

First North American Publication 1995.

PROLOGUE

ARCHER ENTERPRISES, Inc.

Mrs George Cameron
Lilac Hill
Fairview, Illinois

Dear Mrs Cameron,

We received the enclosed letter from Eric Nelson to your late husband this week, and are forwarding it to your attention. Mr Nelson obviously felt that, as George's successors in business, we at Archer Enterprises would always know how to reach George or his family.

Since the letter appeared to be a business communication, I'm afraid the envelope was opened by mistake and the contents read. I have taken the liberty of writing to Mr Nelson to let him know that, sadly, he must have missed the announcement in the trade journals last year of George's death.

Please accept my condolences once more on your loss. I regret that I have not had a chance to pay my respects in person, but next time I'm in the Fairview area I'll consider it an honor to call on you.

Sincerely,

Dillon Archer

Chairman of the Board &
Chief Executive Officer

EHN

Dear George,

You remember me, don't you? We met at a convention once in Chicago and had a great time. I read in the trade magazines that you've sold out and retired, you old fox! What's keeping you occupied now? Building doll-houses for the grandchildren? Well, if so, it's just another kind of box, and you've got plenty of experience after forty years in that business.

If you ever get near Naples, Florida, give us a shout. Martha and I are in the phone book, and we'd love to see you again and talk over old times.

Best wishes,

Eric Nelson

LILAC HILL
BED AND BREAKFAST
FAIRVIEW, ILLINOIS

Hosts:
Geneva Cameron
Heidi Cameron

Mother,
I found this incredible communication as I was going through today's mail, and I thought you ought to see it. Doesn't Dillon Archer have a nerve? He steals Daddy's plant in a hostile takeover and then has the gall to call himself 'George's successor in business'. He actually sends you his condolences—as if it weren't his manipulation that caused Daddy's heart attack! And as for the supreme audacity of offering to pay his respects in person—whenever it's convenient for him—well, I'm just glad the man hasn't set foot in Fairview since the day he got control of the Works, and that he's never likely to...

A TEAR dropped on the note. Heidi wiped it off, but it had already stained the lavender paper.

It was more than a year since her father had died, and most of the time the pain had faded to a dull ache. These letters, however, had brought it back to full heat.

The image Eric Nelson's letter evoked of the way things should have been haunted her. If her father were still alive, he wouldn't be playing with his grandchildren, for there weren't any. But he darned well ought to have been fiddling in his woodworking shop, or playing golf, or visiting old friends.

But George Cameron was dead, and the family business was in the hands of strangers. The whole thing was so damned unfair...

So why upset her mother with it too? Nothing would be gained by distressing Geneva. Wouldn't it be better to pretend the cursed letters had never come?

Heidi wouldn't throw them away, though. She folded both letters and her note and tucked them into a pigeonhole of her desk.

She almost hoped Dillon Archer *did* show up in Fairview some time. There were a whole lot of things she'd like to tell him.

CHAPTER ONE

MITCH sounded as if he was begging. 'You will take good care of him, won't you?'

Heidi Cameron shifted the telephone to her other ear, pulled off her gold button earring, and rubbed the lobe. 'Of course I will, Mitch,' she said soothingly. 'I'll take care of your prospect just as tenderly as you would if you were here—if you ever let me get off the phone and over to the hotel to pick him up!'

Mitch laughed. 'All right, I shouldn't have asked. But you know how much I'd love to be there, showing him what a great town Fairview is, and how perfect it would be for his new plant.'

'I'll show him,' Heidi said, and put the phone down. She gave her dark brown hair a shake, grabbed her forest-green jacket from the doorknob, and paused in the outer office. 'Betty, I'm going to pick up Mr Masters at the hotel and take him to the ribbon-cutting at the new craft store. After that we'll be at the Ambassadors' luncheon at——'

The secretary interrupted. 'Masters, the chicken tycoon?'

'That's the one, though if Mitch hears you referring to his new prospect in those sort of terms I can't imagine what he'll——'

'He called to say he can't make the ribbon-cutting.'

Heidi sat down on the arm of the nearest chair. Masters had arrived in Fairview just last night, to check out the city as a location for the multi-million-dollar chicken-processing plant he was about to build. Now he was can-celling out on the very first activity planned for him.

9

Why? Had something turned him off the city altogether? But how could that be? He'd hardly seen anything of Fairview; he'd even refused Heidi's offer to meet his plane last night, saying he preferred to take a cab and go straight to the hotel.

'He said he'd meet you at Lilac Hill for the luncheon, though,' Betty went on.

Heidi started to breathe again. Maybe he was tired from the trip. Or perhaps he just hated ribbon-cuttings. They certainly weren't her idea of high entertainment, especially since in her official capacity with the Business Ambassadors she'd attended every one in Fairview for the past year.

She felt a bit differently about this one, however, since the proprietor was a friend and the new arts-and-crafts store was something she had long wanted to see. She hoped enough other people felt the same way to keep Callie in business.

Half an hour later, in the neat little storefront on Main Street, the Chamber of Commerce president launched into his usual remarks. Heidi had heard it all before, and she found herself thinking instead about the odds facing a new venture.

Starting a small business in a mid-sized city was a tough road these days. Heidi had good reason to know how much grit, determination, patience and capital was required, for it was just a year ago that she and her mother had opened Lilac Hill as a bed-and-breakfast, offering the occasional catered party on the side. Heidi had no lack of grit, determination, and patience, but she didn't have many illusions left. And capital was still in short supply; her mother had had to put a mortgage on Lilac Hill, but even that hadn't been enough. There was a business loan, too, and Heidi had taken the job with the Ambassadors to help out with the expenses.

Things were getting easier as Lilac Hill's reputation spread and the advertising began to pay off. The business was doing as well as Heidi had expected, considering how new it was. But the property taxes were higher this year, and she hadn't anticipated that the tennis court would need resurfacing or that one of the big oak trees would heave a section of the driveway out of line.

'And a warm welcome to the business community!' the Chamber president boomed.

Heidi joined in the polite applause, and the crowd of well-wishers, most wearing the Ambassadors' standard-issue forest-green jacket, shook hands with their new colleague and wandered out to the street.

In the sudden silence, Callie looked around and gave a long sigh. 'Well, this is the day I've been working toward for years. So where are all the customers who are supposed to be standing in line to get in?'

Heidi recognized the look in Callie's eyes and the edge that lay under her dry tone. Both were sheer panic, born of the sudden realization that she'd gambled everything she possessed on this idea and it was too late to back out. Heidi had seen the same look in her mirror and heard the same tone in her own voice last year, on the day that Lilac Hill took its first guest booking.

'They'll come,' Heidi said. 'In the meantime, I'd be honored to be your first customer.' She handed over a pack of calligraphy paper and reached for her wallet. She wished she could stay a while, lending a hand and some moral support. But she'd be a bit late for lunch as it was. She hoped Mr Masters wasn't already waiting.

Lilac Hill lay at the very edge of the city limits, so far out that the area seemed more country than town. From the main highway the house wasn't even visible; a tasteful sign pointed the way down a deceptively narrow road, lined with lilac bushes. The blossoms were gone now, but a month ago the whole length of the drive had been heavy with their scent.

Heidi drove slowly down the winding lane, pausing where it turned and widened to reveal a vista that had always been her favorite view of Lilac Hill, and her favorite part of coming home.

The house was the color of earth and grass and stone, but its solid brown brick, white stucco and green slate did not pretend to melt into the land. Instead its bulk, three stories tall in places, spread proudly across a gently sloping hillside. Wings jutted out at unexpected angles, and ornate chimneys stretched skyward. Here and there, bays and open porches were capped by battlemented balconies. Darker brick traced a delicate pattern over the highest walls, breaking up the expanse, and a grinning gargoyle perched above the massive gothic-arched front door.

Far off to the right side of the house she could catch just a glimpse of the small private lake, its cold blue water shimmering under the brilliant midday sun. Behind the mansion she could see the tennis court, the corner of the wing which contained the swimming-pool, and the barn which had once sheltered her mother's horses.

When the estate had been built shortly after the turn of the century, one critic had called its architecture pseudo-Tudor and said it was both ostentatious and gaudy. Heidi supposed the critic was correct; Lilac Hill was still a bit overpowering to the uninitiated. But to her this was simply home—a warm and loving house, full of sunshine and good smells and laughter.

At least it had been only that until a couple of years ago, when her father's business had begun to falter under the threat of a hostile takeover. Then the takeover had materialized and George Cameron's health had begun to fail. Within months, Heidi's father was dead and Lilac Hill was at risk. Still was at risk, because if the gamble they had taken didn't pay off...

It will, she thought. It has to. For Mother's sake.

Heidi parked her car near the carriage house, away from the dozen vehicles which occupied the brick court at the back of the mansion. Proper manor houses, she remembered her grandfather explaining, didn't have driveways or sidewalks leading to the front door, and so Lilac Hill didn't either. Not that it made much difference, for the back door was nearly as grand, and it led into the same center hall, lined with walnut paneling.

She walked into the solarium, where the murmur of voices beckoned, and ran an appraising eye over the room. Round tables, each skirted with a gaily flowered cloth and set for four, were set up by each of the tall arched windows, in order to provide the best views of the garden just behind the house. Off to one side, the buffet table was already set up, and everything was in place.

She started to look around for Mr Masters. Mitch wasn't very good at descriptions, but fortunately she knew all the Ambassadors, male and female; picking out the one strange man would be simple.

Some of the Ambassadors had already chosen tables, others were standing, drinks in hand. She moved easily around the room, greeting each group.

The stranger was at the last table, in the far corner of the sun-room. His back was toward the window, and he'd tipped his head a little as he talked to the man beside him. At the very moment Heidi saw him, he turned toward her, and sunlight fell soft across his tanned face and gleamed blue-black in his hair.

He was good-looking, but not classically handsome—his features were a little too strong for that. But in any case his looks had little to do with his attraction. He seemed to emit energy that pulsed over Heidi in waves, robbing her of all ability to breathe. She'd felt that way only once before in her life, one summer day down on the lake when she was ten and had caught a wayward canoe paddle right across the solar plexus.

Why hadn't Mitch at least told her that Masters was a sexy devil?

Because Mitch wouldn't have noticed. And she shouldn't, either. He was a business prospect, that was all.

For heaven's sake, she told herself, breathe!

He was talking to Ken Ferris, who managed the Wood Works. That was unfortunate, but it couldn't be helped. Despite its troubles in the last couple of years, the Works was still the biggest employer in Fairview. The business community could scarcely shut Ken Ferris out, and neither could Heidi—even though the Wood Works was owned by Archer Enterprises now instead of the Cameron family. She just hoped Ken hadn't told Masters anything negative about Fairview.

Where Archer Enterprises was concerned, she thought drily, there was no predicting what might happen.

Her prospect didn't seem to be listening to anything Ken Ferris was saying, however. He hadn't taken his eyes off Heidi, and as she approached he raised his index finger to touch the corner of his mouth.

Involuntarily she licked her lower lip, and saw his eyes brighten.

It's absolutely sizzling in here, she thought. I knew we should have had this party in the dining-room, where the air-conditioning is more easily controlled.

He rose, with slow grace. He was even taller than she'd expected, at least eight inches above her own five-six. 'I don't believe I've had the pleasure,' he said. His voice was deep but surprisingly soft. Just listening to him made Heidi think of slipping down into a warm pool of water and drifting away.

'Welcome to Fairview,' she managed. Mercifully, her voice didn't crack. 'I'm glad to meet you, Mr Masters.'

'I'm not,' he said.

'What?' Somehow he'd gotten hold of her hand, and he was holding it close to his chest, almost over his heart. Heidi stared at her fingers, bemused by the sensations which rippled up her arm—warmth, and an almost electrical thrill.

'I'm not Mr Masters. Though at the moment I wish that I were. If he rates a greeting like that...'

Ken Ferris cleared his throat. 'I'm sorry,' he said. 'Let me introduce you. Heidi Cameron, Dillon Archer.'

The black and white marble floor seemed to rock under Heidi's feet.

Dillon Archer...the man who had wrecked her family's business and thereby devastated her father's health and cost him his life—and done it all so casually that he hadn't even bothered to set foot in Fairview to see the company he was taking over.

And now Dillon Archer was standing in the solarium Heidi's great-grandfather Wood had built, as arrogantly as if he owned it as well as the business which had provided the money to build this house. He was still holding her hand, and he was looking at her with a peculiar warmth in his eyes, as if he'd like to taste her...

She jerked away from him. 'My mistake,' she said tightly.

Ken Ferris chuckled nervously. 'I wanted to talk to you anyway, Heidi. You see, I told Dillon about Lilac Hill, and how it's the best place to stay in Fairview, and——'

'Sorry, Mr Archer,' Heidi said curtly, and didn't care that she couldn't have sounded less regretful if she'd tried. 'We're booked solid. Try the hotel.'

She turned on her heel and headed for the table in the far corner, the furthest possible from Dillon Archer. She thought she heard him give a soft little whistle, but it could have just been her ears ringing with embarrassment.

Her face was burning as well. Of all the idiotic things to do, to walk straight up to Dillon Archer like a lovesick cow...

And what was he doing here, anyway? What had brought him to Fairview? If he hadn't even bothered to look at the plant before taking it over...

Of course he hadn't bothered, Heidi thought scornfully. What he had paid for the Wood Works was no more than pocket change to Dillon Archer, so naturally he'd showed no more concern for the purchase than if he'd sent someone out to get him a sandwich.

More importantly, to Heidi at least, was the question of why Dillon Archer was at Lilac Hill in the first place. Ken Ferris was a member of the Ambassadors, of course, but what incredible bad judgement had led him to bring his boss along to this meeting? And to suggest that Dillon Archer might actually stay there—under the roof of the very people he had nearly cheated out of house as well as livelihood...

Heidi chose a chair that would let her keep her back to him, and she held her spine so straight even her grandmother would have been impressed. Just because she'd been forced to open her home to strangers, to serve club luncheons in the solarium and house paying guests in the bedrooms, it did not mean she had to associate with Dillon Archer!

Heidi's mother appeared in the doorway and looked around. There was a fretful line between her brows, and that was so unlike Geneva Cameron that Heidi jumped up and rushed toward her. But it was foolish to think she could protect her mother from their inconvenient guest. Geneva might have encountered him already; someone had no doubt shown him and Ken Ferris the way to the solarium. He might even have sought her out, to offer the condolences he'd promised in that letter last fall...

Then Heidi spotted the man at her mother's side, a short, barrel-chested fellow in a plaid sports jacket. 'You must be Mr Masters,' Heidi said, and offered her hand.

He gave her a sharp look as if considering whether he should admit it, and then nodded. Heidi led him toward the corner table, where two empty chairs remained.

It was the longest business lunch she could ever remember. Fortunately the other two men at their table kept the conversation going, quizzing Masters about his business. One of them even offered to take him to dinner that night. Heidi tried to hide her relief when he accepted the invitation.

She tried to listen to the speaker, but she couldn't concentrate. Her eyes kept straying to the far corner of the room. Not that Dillon Archer was doing anything to attract attention; as far as Heidi could tell, he hadn't even moved since the speaker took the podium. He was merely sitting there, arms folded, legs comfortably extended and crossed at the ankle, to all appearances enjoying both the sunshine and the speaker...

But she could still feel the energy in him. The sensation was milder, at this distance, but it was definitely still there.

He's like a spring, she thought suddenly, wound tight and ready for action, just waiting for a touch to set him free.

He turned his head just then, and smiled at her.

Heidi put her chin up a fraction and leaned toward Masters. 'Is there anything you'd particularly like to see while you're in Fairview?' she asked quietly.

He nodded. 'There is one thing. I'd like to tour your biggest industry. The Wood Works, I believe it's called.'

The speaker finished, and Heidi automatically joined in the applause. Chairs scraped as the Ambassadors rose, but she didn't hear them. 'Why would you want to?' she asked with honest curiosity. 'It's not similar to your business at all. They make boxes.'

Even as she said it, she could almost hear her father exclaiming in shock at the oversimplification. The Works dealt in packaging containers of all sorts, from cereal cartons to shipping crates.

Masters grinned. 'And we use boxes to ship our product—lots of boxes. In fact, I've bought some from this plant, so I'd like to see how it operates. Besides, do you think my competitors in the meat-packing industry invite me in for tours? Hardly—no more than I welcome them into my place of business. But I've found that in principle one assembly line is pretty much like another. No matter what the end product is, there's something to be learned from the process.'

Take care of my prospect, Mitch had told her. That certainly implied showing Masters whatever he wanted to see. But it also meant she was responsible for presenting Fairview in the best possible light, and Heidi wasn't so sure a tour of the Wood Works would be such a great idea. The Works was no longer the showplace it had once been. Ever since Dillon Archer had taken it over, the trend had been down—production had slumped, employment numbers had sagged...

'You can arrange that, can't you?' Masters' voice had a sharp edge.

The man was thinking of investing millions of dollars in this community. He had a right to ask questions before making his decision, and checking out the business climate was a perfectly reasonable request. If seeing the Works turned him off...well, that wouldn't be her fault. It would be just one more thing to lay at Dillon Archer's door.

Besides, she couldn't prevent him from walking across the room to Ken Ferris, or Dillon Archer himself, and asking for a tour.

'I think so,' Heidi said. 'Let me see what I can do.'

She left Masters chatting with the speaker and took a deep breath before she crossed the room again. To all appearances, Dillon Archer was absorbed in conversation with the vice-president of the Chamber of

Commerce. But she suspected he wouldn't be surprised when she turned up at his elbow. She could feel the vibrations he was giving off; no doubt from his perspective it worked something like radar.

She was right; as she joined the group Dillon Archer was saying, 'Thanks for the invitation, but I don't think I'll be in Fairview long enough to make a good Ambassador.' He didn't even look at Heidi, but he raised his hand as if to take her elbow and draw her into the circle.

Heidi side-stepped, and his fingers closed on air. He smiled just a little. 'Well, hello again. Have you reconsidered your decision about renting me a room?'

'I only wish I could,' she said mendaciously. 'Actually, I need to talk to Ken. We have a visitor who wants to see the Works in operation. Can you arrange a tour for him this afternoon?'

Ken's glance at Dillon Archer was so fleeting that Heidi almost missed it. It puzzled her a bit; Ken was the plant manager, for heaven's sake—why would he feel he needed Dillon Archer's permission to arrange a simple tour?

But it was Dillon who answered. 'I think we can accommodate the lady, don't you, Ken? On condition that she comes along to keep her protégé in line, of course.'

Heidi opened her mouth to protest. Masters didn't need a chaperon. Besides, she hadn't been in the plant since her father had packed up the contents of his desk, and she didn't want to see what Dillon Archer had done to it.

Dillon was watching her lips as if he was already certain of what she'd say and was merely waiting for the opportunity to withdraw the carrot he'd dangled in front of her. But then she'd be in a jam with Masters, and with Mitch when he came back...

'Fine,' she said curtly. 'What time?'

Ken said uncertainly, 'Half an hour?'

'I'll see you then.' Heidi turned on her heel and walked away, uncomfortably aware that Dillon Archer was smiling.

She felt a pang of disloyalty as she approached the old brick administration building precisely half an hour later. It wasn't that she'd taken a solemn vow never to set foot in the Works again, but to go inside that plant as a guest of Dillon Archer—a self-invited guest, to be sure, and an unwilling one, but a guest nevertheless— seemed an insult to her father's memory.

The guide who came to greet them was a long-time employee, one Heidi remembered from years ago and who obviously remembered her. She shook his hand warmly. 'How are things going, Jack?'

He shot a look at Masters and said diplomatically, 'Hard to tell, Miss Cameron. Lower production among our customers means fewer things to ship, and less need for packaging. Times are tough all over, you know.'

He gave the standard spiel about the plant's products and its market area, and handed out safety glasses before leading the way into the factory.

Heidi took one look down the length of the first building and gasped. Everybody in Fairview knew that the Works no longer employed as many people as in her father's day. But what she hadn't realized was that much of the machinery was gone as well. The huge building, once bustling with workers and crammed with huge cutters and folders and presses, now held just one row of equipment, and the sounds of manufacturing echoed from the empty corners.

Masters looked at her curiously, but he didn't ask why she had reacted so strongly. Instead he turned to the guide. 'Why's it called the Wood Works, anyway? Almost everything you do is in corrugated cardboard, isn't it?'

The guide nodded.

Another voice said, 'Perhaps Miss Cameron can answer that question better.' Dillon Archer appeared beside her.

It was only then Heidi realized that she'd breathed a sigh of relief when they'd left the administration area for the factory floor—safe, she'd thought, from his presence. She ought to have known better, of course. Though why the man would want to follow her around…

He obviously had no trouble reading the question in her face. 'I haven't had the tour myself,' he said smoothly. 'Not the official one. I think it's always a good idea to check out what the public's being told about one's business, just to make sure it's all consistent.'

The comment was reasonable enough, but Heidi didn't believe it. She shrugged it off, however, and answered Masters' question. 'The company was founded by Horace Wood right before the turn of the century, and passed down through the generations—to his son Frederick, then to Frederick's son-in-law. So it's always been called the Wood Works. Kind of catchy, I always thought.'

'But it's not still in the family,' Masters pointed out.

'No,' Heidi said. 'No, it's not still in the family.'

The guide gave her a sympathetic look and drew Masters off toward a press which put creases into sheets of cardboard so a box would fold just right.

'I'm very sorry about your father,' Dillon said.

She couldn't look at him. Of course he was sorry, she thought. Only a monster would deliberately cause that sort of suffering; Dillon Archer simply hadn't anticipated the results of his actions. But that fact didn't relieve him of responsibility where George Cameron was concerned.

He seemed to know that pursuing the topic would only make things worse, and he didn't say a word for the next three minutes. Then, while Masters was admiring a job drawing tacked up over a work station, Dillon said, 'Ken was telling me about the Ambassadors.'

'Really?' Heidi hoped he heard the chill in her voice.

'He thinks it's a very unusual organization.'

'He's right.' She didn't elaborate.

Dillon seemed to take the hint, and they walked along in silence down the length of the building and on into the next one, where company names and logos were printed on to boxes. Here, too, machinery that Heidi remembered from her childhood was missing.

'What did you do with it all?' she asked finally.

'The presses? Sold some, junked the others.'

'And you haven't replaced them with anything? No wonder employment is down so far.'

'The machines were out of date.'

'And what about the people? Were they out of date too?'

He frowned. 'We haven't eliminated anyone's job.'

'With a few exceptions. Or have you forgotten?' She was thinking about her father's assistant manager, who had been gone within days of the takeover.

'Surely you can't blame me for wanting my own management team? But as far as the line employees, we haven't cut a single position. We simply haven't hired replacements, so as people retire or seek other opportunities——'

'Which of course they're doing, because they know there's no future here. I'm surprised you haven't closed the plant down. Or are you just waiting till you can depreciate the whole thing for the tax advantages, and then you'll abandon it?'

'Heidi——'

'I don't recall suggesting that you use my first name.'

He let the silence lengthen, and said finally, with surprising mildness, 'Perhaps we'd be better off talking about the Ambassadors after all.'

'I thought you wanted to take part in the tour.'

He nodded toward Masters and the guide, well off to the side with their heads practically inside a machine.

'Somehow I doubt this is anything like the standard tour the schoolchildren get.'

'Of course not—Mr Masters is a prospective customer. Shouldn't you be paying more attention to him?'

'Oh, I wouldn't want him to feel pressured.'

'Then surely there's something back in the administration building that's crying out for your attention.'

'Don't you think that's Ken's job?'

Heidi was exasperated. 'Why are you even here in Fairview, anyway?'

'Are you seriously suggesting I owe you an explanation?'

She turned away. Moisture stung her eyes, but the heavy plastic safety glasses prevented her from discreetly wiping it away. She blinked fiercely instead.

Obviously he wasn't going to go away, and she couldn't—short of pretending a faint or something similar, and she knew darned well Dillon Archer wouldn't be fooled by that. So she said, 'The Business Ambassadors started out as just another boosters' club. You know the kind of thing—pancake breakfasts, barbecue suppers, a scholarship drive now and then. But a few years ago some far-sighted people began to think that it wasn't wise for a city the size of Fairview to depend so heavily on one major industry. A wise decision, from the looks of things.' She waved a hand at the depleted production line.

She didn't know what kind of response she'd expected, but he merely looked interested.

'So they reorganized and started sending people out to recruit industries that were looking for expansion possibilities. They were successful on a small scale, so they took on bigger challenges. Eventually they hired a full-time recruiter—that's my boss—and started...'

'You work for the Ambassadors? You're not just a member?'

Heidi nodded.

'But I thought you ran the bed-and-breakfast.'

'My mother and I do. But I owe the community something as well.'

'I see,' Dillon said thoughtfully. 'You're suffering from a touch of lady-of-the-manor syndrome. I expected as much.'

Heidi bit her lip. There was nothing to be gained by getting into a childish shouting match; to do so would only encourage him to delve further into her reasons for working, and she'd just as soon he did not know how things were going at Lilac Hill. It was none of his business.

The tour seemed to go on forever, and they finished it in icy silence. Back at the administration building, Masters offered a perfunctory 'thanks'.

Heidi smiled at the guide, then fixed her gaze on Dillon Archer's tie and said politely, 'I appreciate the trouble you took.' Which, of course, was precisely none, and she didn't think he'd miss her implication.

'How kind of you to mention it,' he said gently. 'If I should find myself needing a favor in return——'

Heidi's temper snapped. 'If you think this means I owe you one——'

'Of course it does. But you needn't hold your breath. I make it a point never to blackmail a lady.'

Masters was silent almost all the way across town to his hotel. Heidi hardly noticed, till he said finally, just as she pulled up at the main entrance, 'It doesn't look like a terribly profitable operation, does it?'

She was startled, at a loss for an answer that would be both diplomatic and true. But Masters didn't seem to care whether she replied.

'Yes, I think Archer might be open to negotiations,' he mused. 'Considering the circumstances, I might get very favorable terms. If I decide to come here, that is.' He gave her a crooked smile and patted her arm. 'I'll tell Mitch you were a great deal of help, if it all works out. Now, can I buy you a drink, little lady?'

Heidi turned him down as gently as she could, pleading the need to get back to Lilac Hill. She wasn't telling even a white lie; all she wanted to do was go home.

She had never been so happy to see Lilac Hill, or so relieved that tonight there would be no guests. The house was not overflowing with guests, as she'd told Dillon Archer. Far from it, in fact; this was one of the rare days when they had no bookings at all.

I never expected to be grateful for that, she thought. No guests meant no cash flow. But it also meant quiet and relaxation and a chance to feel that she was at home again—home as it used to be. And tonight that was a very precious sensation indeed.

She went straight to her room on the top floor to shower and change clothes. She considered her wardrobe and settled on brief shorts and a co-ordinating top. She didn't bother with shoes; she enjoyed the feel of Lilac Hill's mellow hardwood floors beneath her toes.

On a day like today, with no guests on hand, there would be no formality. The housekeeper would be in her apartment above the carriage house, putting her feet up for a well-deserved rest. Geneva and Heidi would relax with a drink and then simply help themselves to the leftovers from the Ambassadors' party.

There hadn't been time or privacy to talk to her mother after lunch, so Heidi still didn't know how Geneva felt about Dillon Archer's appearance. Had he mentioned that letter?

The stereo was playing in the library, which they had always used as an informal sitting-room. The music was Rachmaninov, a moody piece. Geneva was feeling melancholy, Heidi deduced. As well she might...

She didn't feel the vibrations till she was past the door, and then it was too late, for Dillon Archer was rising from the wing-backed chair by the empty fireplace. 'Your

mother said you'd be coming soon to keep me company.'
His gaze skimmed from her still damp hair to her bare
toes, lingering appreciatively over the length of her legs.
'May I get you a drink?'

Heidi's skin felt as if she'd gotten too close to a blow-
torch. She said irrationally, 'There were no cars out
behind the house when I came home.' Had he just arrived, then? Perhaps he'd only dropped in to pay a con-
dolence visit as he'd promised to do...

Dillon frowned as if he shared her puzzlement. 'As a
matter of fact, I noticed that too. Do your guests often
arrive so late? Or have they all just happened to cancel
their reservations since lunchtime?'

Heidi was caught, and she knew it. She swallowed
hard.

Dillon took a step closer. 'Isn't it fortunate for me
that I talked to your mother this afternoon and found
there was a room available after all?'

CHAPTER TWO

'WHERE *is* my mother?' Heidi snapped.

'I haven't the vaguest idea. She brought me in here, showed me the bar, and apologized for leaving me to my own devices.' Dillon picked up a crystal glass from a small table beside the wing-backed chair.

The contents looked like Heidi's father's favorite Scotch. That was just one more bit of salt in the wound. Dillon Archer, staying at Lilac Hill, drinking George Cameron's Scotch...what had Geneva been thinking of?

'How about that drink?' Dillon asked. He'd moved to the little bar, fitted craftily inside a shallow closet that was usually concealed by a rank of bookshelves.

Heidi shook her head.

He shrugged and topped off his own glass. 'Are you always so liberal with your guests, giving them the run of the house and the bar like this?'

Heidi was too shaken to consider the benefits of being tactful. 'Not generally. But perhaps Mother couldn't stand being in the same room with you.'

The insult bounced off him without visible effect. 'I doubt that, or she wouldn't have invited me to take pot luck for dinner.'

What in heaven's name *had* gotten into Geneva? The sooner this was sorted out the better. Without even murmuring an excuse, Heidi turned on her heel and headed for the kitchen.

Her mother was perched on a high stool at the breakfast-bar with a pastry bag, piping mashed potatoes around the edge of a pottery dish. She looked up with a bright smile. 'Hello, darling.'

'Mother, what are you up to?'

'This? It's just turkey beaulieu, made from the leftovers. I thought it would make a nice change. And since we have a guest tonight after all...'

'I know,' Heidi said grimly.

'Oh. Well, don't you think something other than shorts would be more appropriate?'

'Mother, why on earth would you rent a room to Dillon Archer?'

The housekeeper turned from the sink where she was washing lettuce. 'Because his money's as good as anyone else's, that's why.'

'That's a matter of opinion, Kate.'

Kate sniffed. 'And my opinion is pride's an expensive luxury when you haven't any cash.'

Geneva looked so unhappy that Heidi's irritation drained away. She put a comforting arm around her mother's shoulders. No matter how much she disagreed with Geneva's logic in this particular case, Heidi had to admit that her mother was trying her best to make a go of Lilac Hill. And though turning the house she loved into a commercial enterprise had been a tremendous blow to Geneva's pride, she had never once complained.

'I couldn't help but think of what you said, Heidi—that it takes half of our rooms rented every day just to cover our expenses. And today, without even one guest... Well, when Dillon called, I just couldn't square it with my conscience to turn down a customer.'

Heidi sighed. The least she could do right now was not to make her mother feel worse. She tried for a good-natured grumble. 'I just hope you're getting a premium price out of him.'

Geneva smiled a little and picked up the pastry bag again.

The oven timer chimed. Kate opened the door, shut it again, and gave the timer another twist. The tangy scent of sausage and tomato drifted through the kitchen.

'Are you making hors d'oeuvres?' Heidi demanded. 'Since when does anybody get that kind of service around here?'

Kate glared at her. 'Run up and put on something decent,' she ordered.

Heidi had been taking orders from Kate since she was old enough to walk, but this one was too much. 'You can coddle him if you like, Kate, but if you think I'm changing clothes for that man you're wrong. It's my night off and I'm going to be comfortable.' Then, a bit too late, she remembered the way Dillon had looked at her and thought she might feel less scorched if she took Kate's advice and changed into something less revealing.

Oh, let him look, she thought stubbornly. That was all the satisfaction he'd get.

So she stayed in the kitchen, helping cut up garnishes for the salad Kate was making and watching as Geneva finished trimming a half-dozen ramekins with mashed potatoes. The meal would be nothing fancy—not by Lilac Hill standards, at any rate—but it was far above the pot luck Geneva had modestly offered. Heidi hoped Dillon had the good taste to appreciate the effort that was going into his dinner.

The chime sounded again, and Kate yanked out a pan of tiny sausage pizzas just as the crust reached a perfect shade of brown. She slid them expertly on to a china plate and thrust it toward Heidi. 'Here. Take these in to Mr Archer.'

'*Definitely* a premium price,' Heidi muttered as she picked up the plate.

She thought Kate looked a little surprised that she hadn't argued over being sent on an errand, but Heidi didn't intend to stick around and explain her motives. She certainly wasn't eager to share Dillon's company, but since she was going to have to be polite to him in her mother's presence she was determined to make sure he didn't misunderstand and think she'd had a change of heart.

Dillon had moved to the window-seat and was dreamily looking out over the expanse of smoothly mown lawn at the front of the house. He showed no sign of having heard the whisper of Heidi's bare feet on the oak floor, and she was almost directly behind him when he spoke. 'Am I staying?'

Heidi's brow furrowed. She set the plate down within his reach and perched at the far end of the window-seat. 'I thought you and Mother had already decided that.'

'In principle, yes. But she suggested I ask you about rates, since you're the businesswoman of the enterprise. And of course until I know what this is going to cost me...'

Could he still be discouraged, then? Maybe she could get out of this yet. Heidi couldn't quite meet his eyes, so she picked out a diamond-shaped piece of leaded glass in the window just above his shoulder and quoted him a price which was three times the usual rate for their most expensive room.

He didn't flinch. 'You'll take a credit card at the end of my stay, of course?'

Heidi was disappointed. She'd expected him to argue, at least. The price was outlandish for Fairview—though perhaps Dillon didn't know that. She wished she'd multiplied by five instead. 'That depends on how long you're here, of course. If it's going to be longer than a few days we'd appreciate periodic payment.'

He didn't take the hint. 'At the moment, I haven't the vaguest idea how long I'll be staying.'

So much for that attempt to smoke him out. Heidi tried to visualize the calendar on her desk upstairs. Too bad they didn't have a single day coming up without a vacant room; it would be sheer pleasure to have an iron-clad excuse to kick Dillon out.

He offered her the plate; Heidi shook her head.

Dillon savored a tiny pizza. 'These are very good.'

Pure perversity made Heidi say, 'I hope you understand that the price I quoted you doesn't include dinner.'

His eyebrow arched slightly. 'Oh? And how much extra is that going to cost me?'

'Nothing. You were invited out of the goodness of Mother's heart.'

'I'm touched.'

'I just want to make it clear that you shouldn't expect that service to continue. We don't usually provide evening meals for guests—that's why the whole industry is called bed-and-breakfast.'

'I'll keep it in mind,' Dillon said politely. 'Why are you running a bed-and-breakfast, anyway?'

As if the man had no idea that the Camerons might be in need of money! But of course, Heidi reflected, it had probably never occurred to him to wonder how they would manage on the pittance he had paid for the Works.

Her voice was tart. 'Isn't it obvious? We took stock of our assets, which included a whole lot of bedrooms and a talent for making people feel at ease and at home.'

'*Your* talent, you mean?' His voice held considerable irony.

Heidi felt her cheeks flush. It wasn't her fault that Dillon brought out the absolute worst in her, was it? Normally, she was nearly as good a hostess as Geneva was. She was every bit as concerned about her guests' comfort, and just as able to look after their needs. 'My mother was trained from the cradle to take care of guests, and she does it beautifully.' Heidi could feel a catch in her voice; she hoped he hadn't heard it. 'If you don't mind, I'd rather not discuss it any more. Why aren't you having dinner with Ken Ferris, anyway? I'd think if you only got into town today, you'd have business to discuss.'

'I believe in conducting business during business hours.'

'And pleasure the rest of the time? Well, I hope you enjoy yourself at Lilac Hill.' She stood up. 'If you'll excuse me...'

'You aren't going to stay and entertain me?'

'Look, Mr Archer——'

'Dillon,' he said quietly. He rose too, and suddenly the path she had intended to take was blocked.

There were other ways out of the room, but Heidi had the silliest feeling that dodging him wouldn't do any good. That was ridiculous, of course—he couldn't possibly hold her prisoner in a room that size. Still, she stood her ground and faced him rather than edging around the leather couch to the door.

'I have to get along with you,' Heidi said. 'I don't have to like you.'

'That's all right. Liking isn't precisely the word I had in mind, anyway.' Dillon drew a casual finger down the side of Heidi's face, tracing the hairline from brow to ear, then sliding softly down the length of her throat.

She couldn't quite suppress a shiver.

'What do you call that, Heidi?'

'How about loathing?'

Dillon smiled. 'No,' he said softly. 'Oh, no.'

Then he stepped aside and gave a mocking little bow, and let her go.

One of Geneva's household rules was that no matter how simple the food it should be presented with pride. Heidi had heard her mother say it a hundred times, so she shouldn't have been surprised to see the dining-room table set with her great-grandmother's Havilland china and the gleaming silver candelabra which had been a wedding gift to Geneva.

Heidi slid into her own chair while Dillon was still assisting her mother. She knew he was amused by her haste, but he said only, 'Robbing me of the chance to be a gentleman, Heidi? How inconsiderate of you!'

Heidi had to bite her tongue to keep from answering, and of course he saw that too. While Geneva murmured grace, Heidi stared at her fruit cup as if fascinated by the maraschino cherry on top. She could still feel his touch on the side of her face, and she didn't want to see the ironic humor in his eyes.

But she had herself under control once more by the time Geneva shook out her napkin and picked up her spoon.

'How long do you plan to be in Fairview, Dillon?' Geneva asked.

Dillon let the silence draw out.

He probably thinks I put her up to asking, Heidi concluded. And so what if he did? It was still a reasonable question. She looked directly at him with a polite little lift of her brows.

Dillon smiled and said deliberately, 'Until I've fully enjoyed everything the city has to offer.' His eyes held a wicked gleam that swept Heidi's breath away.

He might just as well have come straight out and said he'd like to entertain himself with me, she thought. The pure and simple gall of the man astounded her.

Geneva, who hadn't intercepted the look, took the statement at face value. 'Then you'll be busy for a long time,' she said. 'Fairview is an amazing city, for its size. We have a very good dinner theater, and a symphony orchestra...'

Dillon listened with apparent interest as his hostess chatted on. But he scarcely took his eyes off Heidi.

'...and of course all the advantages of two colleges,' Geneva went on, 'which is really very unusual for a city this size. One of them specializes in technical training tailored to the employer's needs, and I understand the programs are outstanding. If you're ever in need of specialized training at the Works...'

'I'll keep it in mind,' Dillon murmured.

Geneva went on, 'And of course the liberal arts college is magnificent. That's where Heidi got her degree. Her first one, that is. She was working on her master's when George died.' Geneva's eyes clouded a little.

Heidi was worried. The perfect hostess seemed to be slipping a little. 'Mother...'

Kate came in just then to clear the fruit cup and serve the turkey beaulieu and salad. Heidi was grateful for the bustle and distraction.

Dillon said, 'A master's? In what field?'

Heidi lifted her chin. 'I was doing my thesis on medieval paper-making techniques.'

She thought he was going to choke. 'Oh, that sounds like a thriving field. I'll bet you had employers standing in line waiting to hire you.'

'Must you be condescending?' Heidi said crossly. So what if her field of study had been esoteric? Her father had always encouraged her to follow her dreams—and a few years ago, when she'd chosen her specialty, there had been no reason to suspect she might actually need to make a living at it. By the time Heidi realized the Works was in danger, it had been too late to change her major. She'd have had to start almost from the beginning. Then, when her father died and they knew how bad things really were...

Geneva cleared her throat. 'Heidi does beautiful bookbinding. You may have noticed some of her volumes in the library.'

'I'll make it a point to look,' Dillon promised gravely.

Heidi decided it was time to signal her boredom with the whole subject. 'I think it's going to rain.' The section of sky she could see through the dining-room's bow window was unusually dark, and the big trees tossed in the rising wind.

'There have been storm warnings,' Geneva agreed. 'Perhaps after dinner you should put your car in the carriage house, Dillon.'

'That's very thoughtful of you. Won't you tell me more about Fairview, Geneva?'

Heidi hardly listened. She toyed with her turkey beaulieu and wondered how long this meal could possibly go on. At least she'd had the sense to make clear to Dillon that he wasn't going to be joining them for dinner every evening.

When Kate brought in peach pie à la mode for dessert, Heidi shook her head.

Dillon tried a bite. 'You're missing a great treat.'

'You can have mine.'

Geneva poured him a cup of coffee. 'Heidi has always preferred a simple piece of fruit to a sweet dessert.'

Oh, please, Mother, Heidi thought. He can't possibly be interested.

Geneva picked up the pot again. 'Coffee, darling?'

'No, thanks, Mother. If you'll excuse me, I want to get to the kitchen before Kate has a chance to start on the dishes. She's had a long enough day as it is.' She saw Dillon's eyebrows go up slightly. 'We all pitch in around here, you see.'

He didn't comment, and Heidi escaped into the kitchen with a sigh of relief. Kate had already run a sink full of steaming soapy water, and it took a bit of persuasion—and finally a direct order to go home before the storm struck in earnest—before she dried her hands.

'As if I'm likely to melt in the rain before I get across the driveway,' she grumbled. 'But if you insist on being bossy, I guess I'll go. Now you hand-wash every bit of that china. No cutting corners and putting it in the dishwasher. You know how Miss Geneva feels about her grandmother's Havilland.'

'*I'm* being bossy? You're a fine one to talk!'

Kate grinned and went out the kitchen door.

Blessed solitude, Heidi thought. It was something she'd never given much thought to in connection with Lilac Hill until they'd started the bed-and-breakfast; in a house that size, quiet and space had never been a problem. In the last few months, however, it had become more difficult to find room—and especially time—to be completely alone. And now, with Dillon Archer in the house...

Two rooms away, she could still feel the man's presence. She couldn't explain the phenomenon, but it felt like the throb of a bass drum, without the sound.

It's just resentment, she told herself. How could any man be so insensitive, anyway—pushing himself in where he so clearly wasn't wanted?

But then, Dillon Archer must always have been short on humanitarian impulses. If he'd had a shred of decency, he'd have bought the Works earlier, while it still had some value. He wouldn't have pushed so hard to drive the plant into oblivion so he could pick up the remaining bits at a bargain-basement price. If Dillon had been reasonable, George Cameron wouldn't have looked pale and haunted for all those months, and he might not have had that final heart attack.

It was a small crumb of comfort that at least Dillon was going to pay well for the inconvenience he was causing. If he stayed a week, Heidi calculated, she'd have more than enough money to take care of the damaged driveway. Two weeks, and she could resurface the tennis court as well.

Of course, two weeks of Dillon didn't bear thinking of, tennis court or no. She'd just have to grit her teeth and get through it day by day, that was all.

Gradually the soothing rhythm and the warm water relaxed her. From the time she was tiny, Heidi had always enjoyed the aftermath of a party. She could remember 'helping' at the age of four, standing on a chair with one of Kate's big aprons swaddled around her, swishing dishes through sudsy water. The first time she'd been trusted with the Havilland was as memorable an occasion as her first boy-girl dance...

'Hello,' Dillon said from the doorway, and Heidi dropped a dinner plate. It slid down into the water and clanked hard against another piece, and her heart went to her throat as she fished it out and inspected the rim. But it had escaped damage. She rinsed it carefully and then looked at Dillon. He was holding a stack of china—the dessert plates and saucers, with the coffee-cups balanced precariously on top.

'I hope Mother didn't see her Havilland stacked that way.' Heidi wiped her hands and took the dishes from him, taking care not to touch him.

'I was very cautious.'

'Thanks. I appreciate your clearing the table, but you really don't have to help.'

'Since I'm not officially a paying customer till bedtime...'

'What?'

'Well, you pointed out earlier that dinner was on the house, so to speak. And a very good dinner it was, too. So...'

Heidi found herself actually feeling a little respect for the man. It was only a smidgen, that was true, and it was grudging. But for an instant she almost liked him. At least he had the decency to appreciate the effort Geneva had made. 'I didn't think you'd take me so seriously about everybody pitching in that you'd start clearing tables.'

His voice was smooth. 'Oh, I didn't. I had ulterior motives.'

Heidi shot a look at him. He smiled and leaned casually against the counter, just far enough from the sink to be safe from sloshing suds, and just close enough for the throbbing sensation of his presence to interfere with her heartbeat.

'You don't say.' Heidi's tone was dry. She didn't need three guesses to know what he meant—she'd been pursued into out-of-the-way nooks and crannies before by men who thought their attractions were irresistible. Considering the way he'd been looking at her over dinner, and that electric touch in the library earlier, it was obvious what he had in mind. She was only surprised that he'd bothered with the dishes; a man so supremely self-confident as Dillon didn't need an excuse to follow her.

Well, let him try to steal a kiss. It would be a positive pleasure to drench him.

'I admit it,' he said easily, and moved a step closer.

Heidi's fingertips sought out the dishcloth.

'I hoped I could swap clearing the table for another cup of coffee.'

Heidi blinked in surprise and dropped the cloth, splashing dishwater over the front of her blouse.

Dillon watched with considerable appreciation as she brushed suds away. 'What's wrong, Heidi?' he asked solicitously. 'Did you think I came out here for something else? Oh, if you really want me to kiss you, I'd be happy to oblige, but . . .' He reached past her for the top cup on the stack of dishes she'd set by the sink. His arm brushed her breast, and Heidi jerked away.

Dillon laughed. He poured his coffee and lounged against the counter with the dainty cup cradled in his hand.

Heidi had to grit her teeth to keep from hitting him with the dishcloth. That hadn't been an accidental touch, but she knew challenging him would get her nowhere. She'd probably be better off to ignore it.

But that was easier said than done. She knew he was watching her; she could feel the warmth of his gaze. She concentrated on the dessert dishes.

'Nice kitchen,' he said finally.

Heidi wanted to ignore him. Surely sooner or later he'd get bored and go away. On the other hand, perhaps she should be grateful he'd changed the subject. If she played along, he'd have no excuse to torment her. 'Daddy remodelled it for Mother as a gift a few years ago.'

He pursed his lips as if to whistle—or blow a kiss—and seemed amused when Heidi hastily looked away. 'It must have been a special occasion.'

Heidi nodded, but she didn't elaborate. It was none of his business that the special occasion had been George and Geneva Cameron's twenty-fifth wedding anniversary, or that the celebration had been the last really big party at Lilac Hill before things started to go wrong.

She let the water drain out of the sink and started to dry the Havilland. Dillon seemed content to watch and drink his coffee. Heidi wondered just how long he intended to stay there, leaning casually against the counter.

'I'm surprised you didn't leave those for the help in the morning,' he said.

'Obviously you don't know my mother. She'd be out here herself rather than leave her best china to the mercies of someone who might not appreciate how precious it is.' Heidi kept her tone light. Why bother to tell him that Kate was the only help they had, and that she'd be busy enough come morning?

Heidi had almost finished drying the dishes when the telephone rang, and she jumped to answer it. It was getting late, but bookings often came in at odd hours.

But it wasn't a customer, just Barry Evans, who had been her father's assistant at the Works. She recognized his voice even before he identified himself. 'Hi, Barry.' From the corner of her eye she saw Dillon move a little as if to make himself more comfortable. A gentleman would have left the room, she thought. But of course there was no point in expecting Dillon to act like one. She said, with only a hint of malice in her voice, 'Of course I can talk. I'm not doing anything important, just dishes.'

'Good. You're always too busy to talk any more.'

Now that was genuine nerve, Heidi thought, coming from a man who had given her a rush, refusing to be discouraged no matter what she did, right up to the point that George Cameron's fortunes had changed. 'So are you, Barry.'

'You've missed me?' It wasn't really a question, though.

Like I miss an aching wisdom tooth, Heidi wanted to say. She might have done it, too, if she hadn't caught Dillon's reflection in the black glass surface of the oven door. 'You didn't come to the Ambassadors' meeting today.'

'I never have time any more. My new boss isn't as far-sighted as your father was about the advantages of civic involvement, you know.'

'Not many people are, Barry.'

'You can say that again. I'll never have another job as good as at the Works. That damned Ferris wouldn't even give me a chance.' He added hastily, 'Not that I'd have worked for that stinking Archer anyway. That's what I called about, you know. Have you heard anything about Dillon Archer being in town?'

'It came to my attention,' Heidi said carefully.

'Well, I thought I should let you know. Wonder what he wants?'

'I haven't the vaguest, Barry.' Except for a whole lot of coffee, she thought, watching from the corner of her eye as Dillon refilled his cup. How could he drink that stuff, anyway? It was black and stale and probably scorched by now from sitting on the warming-tray for an hour or more. Her conscience told her that as a good hostess she should offer to make a fresh pot, but she smothered the nagging little voice.

'He's probably going to roll a few more heads at the Works,' Barry speculated glumly. 'Wonder if that's how the man gets his kicks, going from plant to plant ruining people's lives?'

'Barry——'

'Well, I just wanted to warn you. Gotta go. See you around, all right?'

Heidi put the telephone down, wiped the last few dishes, and hung the towels to dry. 'It's been a long day, so I'm going upstairs,' she said finally. 'Make yourself at home. I'm sure you can find your way to your room when——'

'Actually, I'm not sure I can. You might consider printing a map of this place.'

Heidi closed her eyes and counted to ten. The last thing she wanted to do was escort Dillon to his bedroom door. 'Which room did Mother put you in?'

'I hardly remember. I was only there for a minute, you understand, just putting my bags away.'

If he thought she was going to give him a tour tonight, showing him every bedroom till he found one that looked familiar, he was dead wrong. 'Wasn't there anything about it which made an impression on you?'

Dillon considered. 'The bed had a canopy.'

Heidi was relieved. 'That's the oriole suite.'

'The what?'

'All the rooms are named after birds. It was either that or flowers, and since I wasn't sure how men would react to being put in a room named after a gladiolus or a water lily...' She was chattering, and she hated it when she did that. One thing was plain; the sooner she could get rid of him the better. 'Come on, I'll show you.'

It felt strange to climb the wide stairway with him just a step behind her. At the top, Heidi stopped and pointed down the hallway. 'It's the third door on the left.'

Interesting, she thought, that Geneva had put him in that particular room, not the master suite which was the nicest in the house. Interesting, but not surprising. Geneva might have felt obliged to take Dillon's business, but she had drawn the line at letting him occupy the room she had once shared with her husband.

So why had she given him the room that had been Heidi's instead?

Because it's the next nicest, Heidi thought. It was the obvious choice. She might well have done the same thing herself; after all, it wasn't as if her things were still there.

Dillon seemed hesitant. 'You're not going to come down and be sure everything's all right?'

'Why? Are you afraid of the dark?'

'No, though if you'd like to offer your services as a night-light I'm sure we'd both find the experience...illuminating.'

'Goodnight, Mr Archer!' She started up the narrower stairs which led to her own quarters on the top floor, knowing quite well that Dillon didn't budge from the landing till she was out of sight. And even after he'd gone down the hall to the room that had once been hers, the subtle throbbing that reminded her of his presence didn't fade entirely from her mind.

Heidi wished she'd thought to bring a book to bed with her. She was darned sure it would be a while before she could find sleep.

CHAPTER THREE

THE rain had started before the dishes were done, but the worst of the storm didn't hit until about midnight. It was fierce but brief, and by morning all evidence of it was gone except for the clean-washed air which greeted Heidi as she stepped out the back door.

At least, she thought the storm had left no trace till she saw the apple tree which had stood near the corner of the barn, down the hill from the house, for as long as she could remember. This morning it was standing no longer. Now it was split and torn, and half of it lay on the ground, leaves already wilting. The other half was leaning, almost uprooted by the force of the wind.

Just what I needed, Heidi thought. The tree was not a problem which could be ignored; the rest of it would come down with the next strong wind, and if it fell wrong it would smash into the corner of the barn.

'That was a heavy sigh.' Dillon came to stand beside her.

Was he just looking for a breath of fresh air too, Heidi wondered, or had he followed her? Not that his motivation mattered, really. Whatever had brought him out here, the result was the same for her.

He was dressed for the office, in summer-weight light gray trousers, a white shirt and a subtle striped tie, but no jacket. That surprised her. Fairview was generally a casual sort of place, particularly in summertime, but she hadn't expected Dillon to adopt that trend. Any man who was as perfectly tailored as he was wouldn't allow minor details like heat to keep him from looking his best.

43

And just when had she bothered to pay attention to his tailoring? she wondered.

'Too bad about the tree,' Dillon said.

'Yes. I used to lie on that big horizontal branch and eat apples one after the other. It was one of my favorite retreats.'

'Was it hit by lightning, do you think?'

'I doubt it. There are lightning rods on the barn, so if it struck anywhere close I'd have thought it would be there.'

'That's a barn?'

In other circumstances, Heidi would have been amused by the surprise in his voice. He wasn't the first person to be amazed by the stucco and half-timbered building. 'If you want to get technical, it's a stable—probably the only Tudor-style one in the country. There's even a training ring behind it.'

'You have horses too?'

'Used to.' But then we had to set priorities, Heidi thought, and there was no money to keep them or time to take care of them. And so her mother's horses had been sold, casualties of the crash.

'Lilac Hill is full of surprises,' he said mildly.

She knew he was talking about her, and her heartbeat sped up just a little. In irritation, she told herself.

Kate appeared at the door. 'I was wondering what became of you two. Your bacon and eggs are ready, Mr Archer, just the way you asked for them.'

'Kate, I hope you didn't bother with anything for me. I thought I'd just——' Heidi's half-hearted protest died under the housekeeper's stern look.

'Get in here this minute, young lady,' Kate said, 'and eat your breakfast.'

Without a word, Heidi followed Kate into the house.

At her elbow, Dillon murmured, 'Well, if *that's* the way to handle you...'

'Don't bet on it. I have to stay in Kate's good graces.'

The dining-room table was set for two. Heidi raised an eyebrow at Kate. 'What about Mother?'

Kate swept the covers off the plates. 'I took her a tray.'

'Isn't she feeling well?'

'Just tired. I thought it would do her good to spend the morning in bed with a book. Now sit down, Heidi, so the man can eat his breakfast while it's still hot.'

Dillon was standing patiently beside her chair. Heidi half expected him to do something silly like kiss the nape of her neck as he seated her, but he didn't. She decided he must have meant what he'd said yesterday about doing business during business hours. Well, that was a relief.

He picked up a jacket which lay across a nearby chair, and pulled a wallet from the inside breast pocket. 'Before I forget it...' He counted out a small stack of crisp hundred-dollar bills and pushed them across the table to Heidi.

She eyed the money with trepidation. 'What's this for?'

'Last night and tonight. You did say something about appreciating it if I'd settle my bill periodically.'

'I didn't mean you had to pay every day or two.'

Dillon smiled. 'I don't mind, especially since if I've paid in advance you can't throw me out even if you get a better offer for the room.' He looked admiringly at the picture-perfect plate of bacon and eggs in front of him. 'I must say you do things up well here.'

'Kate's pride won't allow anything else. She does a buffet when all the rooms are full, but with only one guest it's less trouble to cook to order.' That should keep him from feeling too special, Heidi thought. She tried not to look at the pile of cash beside her plate.

'Are you often booked full?'

She toyed with her toast and thought about saying airily that they seldom had vacancies. But it wouldn't be difficult for him to check out the story; either Kate or Geneva would tell him the truth. 'Full, no—not regularly. But neither are most hotels or inns.'

He nodded, as if conceding a hit.

'But we do a solid business. Last night was a real exception.'

'If you've got rooms available next week...'

'I might,' Heidi said cautiously. 'Why?'

'I happen to know some people who would appreciate this quiet atmosphere. I could tell them about Lilac Hill.'

'That's very kind of you, but I don't think we need to hire a public relations person just yet.'

'Oh, I wasn't asking for a commission—or at least not much of one. I'd settle for a smile now and then.'

'Really?' Heidi said earnestly. 'In that case, I'll tell Kate to be friendlier to you from now on.'

He threw back his head and laughed. His eyes sparkled and his face lit up, and Heidi watched him warily. Dillon was even more dangerous than she'd thought. He was positively infectious when he was truly enjoying himself.

The light of pure amusement stayed in his eyes, but his voice sobered. 'I was surprised last night when you went on upstairs.'

'Why? It's not the sort of attic Cinderella was banished to, you know. It's not quite as elegant as the rest of the house, but it's got perfectly nice bedrooms and baths—even a ballroom.'

'A ballroom? You're joking.'

'Well, it's not as grand as the name implies. It's more of a playroom, actually. I used to have all my parties up there when I was a teenager.' Now why had she told him that? He couldn't possibly be interested.

'But since the guest rooms were empty last night...'

Heidi shrugged. 'When we opened for business Mother and I decided to move up to the top floor so we could keep all the regular bedrooms ready to rent at short notice. It would be a nuisance to move up and down.'

'And you're perfectly comfortable up there?'

'Of course.'

He sounded satisfied, though Heidi couldn't figure out for the life of her why he should be. 'Which room used to be yours?'

'Why would you want to know?' Heidi asked coolly. She pushed back her chair and picked up the stack of hundred-dollar bills which lay beside her plate. 'If you'll excuse me, I'll get you a receipt for this.'

When she came back, he'd finished his breakfast and was drinking a second cup of coffee. He took the slip of paper from her, glanced at it, then folded it tenderly and stowed it in his wallet.

As if it were a love letter, Heidi thought. Though in his eyes a tax-deductible business receipt was probably more of a treasure.

She picked up Masters at his hotel and took him to a meeting with the mayor and the city manager. He was in splendid good humor afterwards, and they had an hour to kill before his flight back to the East Coast, so Heidi gave him the standard tour of Fairview. She showed him the prime residential neighborhoods, the parks and playgrounds, the industrial developments, and he voiced approval of it all.

On the way to the airport, however, he lapsed into silence and seemed to be thinking over what he'd seen, so Heidi let her mind drift as well. It would be fun to call Mitch in California and tell him how successful she'd been with his prospect. She'd swear Masters was sold.

As she turned off the main highway toward the airport, Masters cleared his throat. 'There is one more thing you could do for me,' he began. 'I'll be checking on it myself, of course, but having someone locally—sort of underground, as it were—would be very helpful.'

Heidi's internal warning bells were going off with a vengeance. 'What do you mean, underground?'

'I'd like to know what kind of package the city fathers will really offer to get my plant.'

'But I thought you'd discussed all that with them this morning. There's a fairly standard package the city offers to any new business coming in—property tax breaks for a few years, and——'

Masters was shaking his head. 'Negotiations have to start somewhere, and what they offered me this morning is an opening bid. Of course there's a standard package for the average little business, but a plant the size I'm talking about isn't exactly average, now is it?'

Heidi was stunned. The deal the city offered was more than fair, in her opinion.

'No, they'll do better than that,' Masters mused. 'They'll have to, or I'll go somewhere else. The big question is how much better. That's what I want to know—what they're willing to come through with in the end. It'll save me a lot of time and effort to know up front how much of a concession they'll really make, so I can decide if it's worth squeezing them for more than their standard offer or if I should look again at my other possibilities.'

Heidi swallowed hard. 'I don't think——'

He patted her hand. 'Oh, I'll make it worth your while; don't worry about it.'

'You're asking me to spy?'

'No, no, my dear. Just ask around a little. I'm sure you can find out what arrangements they've made with other people. For instance, I'll bet Dillon Archer didn't come to town on the strength of that standard package they told me about this morning.'

He didn't need to, Heidi thought bitterly. All the concessions Dillon had asked for had been made by the Cameron family—by force. The city hadn't come into it at all.

'Though it doesn't look as if he's doing all that well,' Masters said. 'Funny, I'd have thought Archer would figure out a way to turn a profit at anything he did. I'll have to do some investigating before I decide if I should just buy boxes from him or offer to take over his whole operation.'

Heidi stopped the car in front of the terminal, hardly aware of how she'd gotten there.

Masters gave her a crooked smile and pressed his business card into her hand. 'Now, you won't say anything about all this, will you? And remember, just call me here at this number when you find out what I want to know. I'll make it worth your while, and I never forget a favor. In fact, if I do decide to come to Fairview I'll need an executive secretary—how about it, dear? Would you like the job?' He winked at her and got out of the car.

It was a darned good thing he hadn't hung around and waited for an answer, Heidi thought. She suspected that if she'd done what she wanted to and slapped him it might have been the end of any possibility of a chicken plant in Fairview.

Her head ached.

She stopped at the Mexican restaurant to pick up a bag of burritos and went straight to Main Street. In the brand-new craft store, still smelling of fresh wallpaper paste and paint, she found Callie Martin unpacking a shipment in the stockroom.

'Lunch,' Heidi announced, and sat down on the edge of a table. 'I don't know about you, but I need a thera-peutic gab session.'

Callie laughed. 'Hey, I'm the one with grand-opening jitters. What's gotten into you?'

Heidi told her about Masters. 'And then the slime of-fered me a job,' she finished. 'Imagine me as his executive secretary!'

Callie looked thoughtful. 'Look on the positive side, Heidi. You wouldn't need an aerobics class, because you'd stay in shape just running around the desk to get away from him.'

Heidi wadded up a burrito wrapper and threw it at her.

'Though I'd suggest you hold out for vice-president of public relations at least. With all the hazards of working for a man like that, you might as well have a nice title to show for it.' She sobered. 'Seriously, what are you going to do?'

'Tell Mitch.'

'Of course you're going to tell Mitch. But...' Callie chewed her lip. 'You know, it's awfully interesting that Masters came to town at the same time Dillon Archer did.'

'Coincidence.'

'Are you sure of that? It sounds as if they know each other.'

'Why do you say that? They didn't even acknowledge each other at the Ambassadors' lunch. And they're not the kind of combination I'd expect. Masters is loud and crude, and Dillon's satin-smooth. They're like oil and water.'

Callie shrugged. 'So maybe they've done business before. I said they're probably acquainted, not that they're bosom friends. And why you're acting as if I just insulted Dillon Archer——'

Heidi drew back in surprise. 'I'm not. I've said much worse about him myself. If you think I was complimenting him just then, you're wrong.'

Callie looked doubtful.

Heidi unwrapped another burrito. 'Why do you suppose Dillon's in Fairview, anyway? What does your father say? He's been at the Works so many years, he must have an idea what's going on.'

Callie hesitated and then said flatly, 'It's only speculation, you know that. But Dad says it feels bad.'

'Bad?' Heidi frowned. 'Like what?'

'There have been a lot of outsiders around in the last few months—you know, people with clipboards and hard hats who ask questions but never answer any. They've been coming in for months now, one or two at a time, on no regular schedule.'

'I don't get it.'

'He thinks it's supposed to look casual, but there are just too many of them. And now Archer's here himself, looking things over. Dad thinks the plant may be for sale.'

Heidi turned the idea over thoughtfully. 'That's not the worst thing that could happen. Maybe another owner...'

'That's in his optimistic moments, Heidi. When Dad's feeling down, he thinks Archer's just going to close the whole plant. And I'm afraid it makes sense. The buildings are old, the equipment's dated...'

'The little that's still there,' Heidi said slowly. 'Sold some, junked the others', Dillon had told her during the tour yesterday. His tone had been casual. Did he feel the same about the plant itself—that it was expendable, valueless?

It shouldn't be any surprise if he did; she'd asked him herself why he didn't just close the place down. But somehow Callie's analysis made the possibility much more real, and more frightening. Heidi's fingers closed slowly on the burrito, squashing it slowly into mush.

After a moment, Callie tried to laugh. 'Hey, cheer up, pal. Maybe he's not going to close the Works—maybe he just came to get the pieces of the Cameron empire he missed last time around.' She dug into the bag. 'Do you want the last burrito?'

Heidi waved it away carelessly. 'What pieces? There's nothing left of the so-called Cameron empire.'

'Oh, I don't know. There's Lilac Hill.' Callie took a bite and added indistinctly, 'And there's you.'

* * *

Why was it that a careless comment from a friend could cut so much more deeply than the most calculated insult from an enemy? What on earth had led Callie to speculate that Dillon might find anything attractive about Heidi?

Pure devilment, Heidi told herself. Callie was always speculating about someone's love life, with or without evidence. And in this case she had less than nothing to go on. It was only Heidi's guilty conscience that was making her put any weight on the matter.

Yes, she was feeling guilty, she admitted—because before she'd discovered his identity she'd found Dillon terrifyingly attractive.

And now that she knew who he was... Well, she wasn't quite ready to think about how difficult it was to ignore the man, and how her blood turned to steam whenever he was around.

She'd feel better for a little physical activity, she decided. Especially if she could destroy something. So she left the office a little early and went home to tackle the apple tree that the storm had brought down.

There was an unfamiliar car—a black Jaguar—in the courtyard behind Lilac Hill. She hadn't yet seen what Dillon was driving; she'd left this morning before he'd gotten his car out of the carriage house. Or perhaps the vehicle belonged to the guests who were due to arrive this afternoon. At any rate, she met no one as she climbed the narrow stairs to her room.

As she'd told Dillon over breakfast, the top floor was much less elegant than the rest of Lilac Hill. The rooms were smaller and simpler, and the woodwork was simple white-painted pine. The high, narrow dormer windows were a far cry from the wide vistas she'd enjoyed in her old room. The walls sloped at unusual angles because of the high-pitched roof, so there wouldn't have been enough space for Heidi's tall canopy bed even if she'd seriously considered manhandling it up the narrow stairs.

But their new quarters were perfectly comfortable. There was room for Heidi's books and her childhood dolls, and Geneva had brought up the display case which held the porcelain birds and flowers George had given her on special occasions over the years. And at least they were still at Lilac Hill; this was sumptuous luxury compared to a two-bedroom apartment somewhere downtown.

The adjoining bath, which Heidi shared with her mother, still smelled of Geneva's favorite lilac-scented soap. Heidi washed her face and then put on jeans, dug her riding boots out of the back of her closet, and went to the barn to look for the chain-saw. She didn't think she could manage the whole job, but at least she could get the worst of the dangling branches cut.

It took a while to find the saw, and more time to check it over and fill the fuel tank. Just as she reached the tree, Dillon sauntered across the lawn toward her. 'I suppose you're going to do a little sculpting,' he said cheerfully. 'What an amazingly talented woman you are!'

He was wearing faded jeans that fitted his lean hips like a second skin and boots that looked as worn as her own. Somehow, now that he'd shed the sophisticated veneer of the businessman, he was even more disturbing. And puzzling, Heidi admitted. If he'd turned up wearing crisp jeans and shining boots, she wouldn't have been surprised. But the idea of Dillon being so comfortable in casual garb that he'd practically worn his jeans and boots to a thread upset her somehow.

He caught her studying his clothes and confessed, 'I was looking out my window and spotted you coming toward the barn. I thought maybe you'd been fudging this morning about the horses.'

'Why would I?'

'Because somehow I got the feeling you'd rather not ride with me,' he said airily. 'And since your mother

would probably tell you it was bad manners not to invite
me to join you...'

'She'd say it's worse manners to lie. Do you ride?'

'Now and then.'

'The neighbors just up the road have a stable. I'm
sure they'd be happy to have your business.'

'Oh, I'd hate to go alone. Perhaps we can make a date
for this weekend.'

And maybe hell will freeze by Saturday, too, Heidi
thought. But at least she knew now that he was planning
to stay through the weekend. Maybe she should call the
asphalt people tomorrow and get a bid for the work on
the tennis court.

She gave a noncommittal grunt and pulled the starting
rope on the chain-saw. The engine growled but didn't
catch.

'Give me that,' Dillon said, and reached for the saw.
'You'll hurt yourself.'

Heidi held on to it stubbornly. 'I won't. I'm perfectly
capable. It's only a little chain-saw, and I'm just going
to take off the small branches.'

'So tell me what you want done and I'll do it.'

She stood her ground. 'No. I don't have enough in-
surance to take a chance on you sawing off your foot
or something.'

'You want me to sign a waiver? Come on, give it here.'

Heidi shook her head and turned toward the tree,
pulling the rope again. The saw still didn't catch.

But the growl it made kept her from hearing Dillon
coming up behind her. His right arm closed around her
waist, lifting her off her feet and holding her tight against
his chest. Heidi shrieked and kicked, to no avail.

Dillon only laughed and pried the saw out of her hand.
Then he let her slide down till her toes barely touched
the ground; his arm still held her prisoner, trapped firmly
with her back pressed against him.

'Of course if you'd like to keep on fighting,' he said, 'I'll put the saw somewhere safe so we can both enjoy ourselves.'

The intimate throatiness of his voice tickled her ear. Heidi shook her head. 'If you're going to be dictatorial...'

He let her go, though his hand lingered at her waist for a little longer than was necessary to steady her. Heidi stepped away from him just as soon as she could, hoping that he couldn't tell how her knees were trembling. Maybe it was a good thing she wasn't going to be handling that saw, after all.

Dillon was all business, however, as he studied the tree. 'Shall I cut it into fireplace lengths?' he asked. 'You might as well get some good of it.'

She nodded. 'If you insist. Apple makes a nice fragrant fire.'

Dillon's smile was like a flash of sunlight on a drab day. 'You can stack the logs.'

'Gee, thanks.'

The saw started on his first pull, and a couple of minutes later a large branch dropped with a crash. Dillon cut it neatly into two-foot chunks and stood back, the chain-saw purring, to watch while Heidi stacked the pieces neatly at the corner of the barn. His gaze made her feel warm, far more than the exertion did, and she finally protested. 'It's not gentlemanly of you to watch while I work.'

'I'm just making sure you're out of range before I cut another branch,' Dillon assured her.

Personally, Heidi was convinced his attention had far more to do with the fit of her jeans than a concern for her safety.

She stacked the last logs and sat down atop the pile to wait for more. She couldn't help but see the way his muscles rippled as he maneuvered the saw. Small though it was, it took considerable strength to handle it smoothly, and it was almost a relief to go back to stacking the finished logs so she wasn't tempted to admire the easy way Dillon's body moved.

They quickly fell into a rhythm, accompanied by the rise and fall of the chain-saw's throaty purr. The tree shrank, the log pile grew, and the sun crept toward the west.

Geneva was almost beside them before Heidi heard her. 'Haven't you two heard of tree services?' she scolded in the sudden silence when Dillon turned off the chain-saw. She held out a tray with two glasses of lemonade and smiled at him. 'But thank you for helping out. Heidi takes on far too much around here.'

'My pleasure. I needed some exercise.' Dillon set a log upright and dusted off the end to form a makeshift chair. 'It's the best seat in the house, I'm afraid. If we'd known you were coming, we'd have arranged for a cushion.'

Geneva laughed and perched on the log.

Dillon took a glass and dropped to the grass at her feet. 'It's peaceful out here,' he said. 'If it weren't for the house, one could pretend to be a pioneer, chopping wood for the cook stove.'

Heidi shook her head. 'Sorry to burst your bubble, but cook stoves were a modern innovation. The real pioneers used fireplaces.'

He grinned lazily. 'I'm more of a pioneer than I thought.'

'If you like, I'll find you an axe and you can split all this,' Heidi said sweetly.

Geneva ignored the banter. 'That sense of privacy is the reason my grandfather chose this particular tract of land,' she said. 'It was way out past the city limits then, and he sited the house so no matter where other people built he'd never see evidence of their presence. In fact, you can ramble all over the place and not see another house, except in winter when the leaves are gone.'

Dillon asked, 'Will you show me your favorite walk, Geneva?'

She smiled at him. 'Oh, I just go down to the lake. That's not even a hike—no challenge at all. Heidi's a much better guide, because she knows every inch of this place. In fact, when she was a child Kate used to pack her a lunch every morning in the summertime because no one knew where she'd be come noon.'

'Then I'll ask Heidi to be my guide.'

Heidi jumped up and wiped her hands, damp from the cold lemonade glass, on the seat of her jeans. 'Sorry. I haven't time for that sort of thing any more. I think we've done about all we can, don't you?'

Dillon looked at the remainder of the tree. 'Quit before we're finished? Heidi, I'm ashamed of you.' He set his glass back on Geneva's tray and picked up the chainsaw again.

In another half-hour all that remained was a stump scarring the earth, a huge sweet-scented pile of logs, and a neat heap of small leafy branches waiting to be burned. Plus a whole lot of aching muscles, Heidi realized, though she wasn't going to admit that to Dillon, who was moving as easily as ever as he helped stack the final few logs.

He set the last one in place and stood for a moment with his hands on his hips, staring down across the twilight-shadowed hillside to the little lake.

Say something, she ordered herself. You owe him a great deal—you couldn't have done half the work alone. 'Thanks, Dillon,' she said finally. 'Look, if you really do want to explore Lilac Hill...'

'Yes?' His eyes were brilliant.

She looked away abruptly. The way his gaze seemed to cut straight through her was just short of indecent. 'I'll draw you a map or something.' The offer was a far cry from what she'd intended to say, but it was a whole lot safer.

'I'd rather have a personal guide.'

'I told you—I'm busy.'

'I know. I wonder what you'll find as an excuse next time, since you don't have the tree to fuss with any more?' He stooped to pick up the chain-saw. 'Where does this go?'

'In the barn. I'll show you.' She led the way past the box stall which had once held Geneva's Arabian mare and the one where her own dear pony had lived to the tool-room, and pointed to an empty spot on the highest shelf.

She couldn't move aside quite fast enough; when he reached to push the saw into place, he blocked her into place in the narrow room.

He hadn't done it on purpose, she thought, but the effect was the same as if he had. She was so close to him that the sharp scent of fresh sawdust clinging to his shirt tickled her nose. Mingled with the warmth of his body and the freshness of evening air, it produced an aroma more stunningly erotic than any cologne could be.

A deep breath would make her brush against him, so Heidi tried to stop breathing in order to avoid touching off an explosion. But he must have misunderstood and thought her breathlessness indicated anticipation, for once again that strange brilliance sprang to life in his eyes.

His hands came to rest on her shoulders, turning her toward him. 'Do you have time for this sort of thing?' he whispered. Ever so gently, he pulled her into his arms.

Heidi shook her head. She couldn't have spoken for the world, and she wasn't surprised when he ignored such a half-hearted protest.

Heidi braced herself against the plundering, demanding embrace she expected. But Dillon startled her; he held her as though she were a fragile bit of blown glass and he kissed her almost pleadingly, his mouth moving with exquisite softness against hers.

Heidi's muscles started to melt and her resistance faded. Disarmed by his gentleness, helpless to stop herself, she kissed him back. Dillon's arms tightened, and he grew more insistent, nibbling at her lips, tracing her teeth with the tip of his tongue.

Heidi had no idea how much time had passed when he finally raised his head. She only knew she was weak and wobbly, and she needed to lean against the workbench to steady herself.

She saw that the brilliance in his eyes was not diminished in the least—but it had changed somehow. Desire had been softened just a bit by satisfaction.

Knowing she had reacted precisely as he'd expected annoyed her. 'Well, you got your kiss,' she said. Her voice shook a little. 'Are you contented now?'

She didn't expect an answer; it was a throwaway question.

But Dillon raised his hand to her face and traced the line of her mouth with the tip of his little finger, and said, very seriously, 'Oh, no. I can't imagine I'll be satisfied till I've made love with you.'

CHAPTER FOUR

HEIDI was still steaming over the sheer gall of the man late that evening. Maneuvering her into a corner to snatch a kiss was one thing, but coolly announcing his intention to take her to bed was an outrage.

She hadn't bothered to slap him; she'd thought Dillon would probably be amused by such a predictable reaction. But she hadn't spoken to him since, either.

Not that there had been anything particularly noteworthy about that feat. Dillon had gone out to dinner, and by the time he returned their new guest had also come back from her evening out and was telling Geneva every detail about her three children. Mrs Johnson was in the middle of describing her little darlings' sports achievements when Dillon appeared at the door of the library.

Geneva looked up from her needlepoint with a smile. 'Do come and join us for a nightcap, Dillon.'

Heidi was frankly surprised when he accepted. He must have heard their garrulous guest from the hallway, and Heidi would have bet he'd run in the opposite direction. If it hadn't been for the fascination of the flickering fire—the first they'd lit in weeks—she'd have been tempted to desert Geneva herself.

But Dillon graciously acknowledged Geneva's introductions, poured himself an amaretto, and took a chair opposite Heidi's near the fireplace.

The new guest looked at him coyly. 'I do so enjoy staying at bed-and-breakfast places,' she said. 'One meets such interesting people. Don't you agree, Mr Archer?'

'Absolutely, Mrs Johnson.' His gaze didn't leave Heidi's face.

Heidi wished she had a piece of needlepoint so she could bury herself in it and refuse to look at him. Of course, there was a stack of paperwork and bills on her desk upstairs, waiting for her attention, but to get up and leave the moment Dillon came in would only give the man another excuse to be arrogant.

'And what business are you in, Mr Archer?' the guest persisted.

He smiled. 'A very dull one, I'm afraid.'

Mrs Johnson looked puzzled, but Dillon didn't go on. 'Oh,' she said finally. 'My husband is in clothing.' She began to tell Geneva all about it.

Dillon sipped his amaretto and studied Heidi. 'You look beautiful in the firelight.'

'A line that old is unworthy of you.'

'Even if it's true?'

Heidi didn't bother to answer. She uncurled and stood up. 'Shall I freshen your drink, Mother?'

'Thank you, dear. Mrs Johnson, would you like another brandy?'

Dillon was on his feet, reaching for the glasses. 'I'll help.'

The bar was really too small for more than one person to work. Heidi poured the drinks while Dillon lounged beside the bookcase door. In her haste, she tipped a bottle too fast and missed Mrs Johnson's glass.

'What a waste of good brandy,' Dillon said, and took the bottle out of her hand. 'Don't tell me you're nervous because I'm standing here, Heidi. There's no need. You should be flattered.'

Heidi's vow of silence snapped. 'Because you're here, or because you want to go to bed with me? "Flattered" would not be the word I'd choose in either situation.'

'Neither. You should be flattered because I told you the truth. I'm not ashamed of wanting to make love to you, and I see no reason to beat about the bush.'

She watched as he poured the brandy. His hand was absolutely rock-steady. The dim light in the bar cast long shadows across the lean planes of his face and made his eyelashes look even longer and darker than they were.

'I like you, Heidi.' The words were commonplace, but the tone of his voice turned the comment into a caress that sent bits of ice racing down Heidi's spine.

'Your definition of liking is different from mine.'

'Perhaps it is. We'll see, won't we?'

He carried the drinks to Geneva and Mrs Johnson and waited until Heidi sat down again before he took a seat. It wasn't the first time she'd noticed his perfect manners. Not that etiquette was the reason he'd waited to seat himself, she was positive. He'd simply been making sure that no matter where Heidi sat he'd be close enough to annoy her.

But he didn't pester her with conversation, she had to admit. He simply sat there and watched her in the fire-light as if she were an endlessly fascinating movie.

He was conducting a siege, Heidi thought. And it wasn't fair.

She manufactured a yawn and said, 'Mother, if you'll excuse me, it's getting late and I still have paperwork to do.'

She was amazed that Dillon didn't make his excuses too, for the dubious pleasure of walking her up the stairs. Instead, as she was leaving the library, she heard him say, 'Geneva, if I could talk to you for a moment...'

Heidi wondered idly what was on his mind. Then she decided she didn't care, as long as he wasn't so unashamed of his plans for her that he'd confide in her mother.

Heidi was still at her desk in the top-floor ballroom when Geneva came upstairs an hour later. 'Heidi, it's the most wonderful thing!'

Geneva was practically bubbling over, Heidi thought as she looked up from contemplating Lilac Hill's checkbook balance. Well, they were overdue for some really good news.

'Dillon's talked to some people who want to come and stay with us next week.'

They must be the ones he'd mentioned at breakfast, Heidi decided. Why had he gone to Geneva rather than bringing it up again with Heidi? And why was Geneva so excited? Most of a bed-and-breakfast's trade came through referrals by satisfied guests. This was nothing out of the ordinary.

'There are four of them,' Geneva went on. 'Four rooms, I mean. That's half of our space, Heidi. And it's for a whole week.'

At least that explained Geneva's excitement. Half-occupancy guaranteed for a week would help the budget tremendously even at their regular rates. And if Dillon's friends hadn't quibbled about the price he was paying...

'That's not all, dear. They really want to get away from everything, so he asked if we could provide lunches and dinners too. I said of course we could, and——'

'Hold it, Mother. Can you handle all this? I can't count on being able to get out of the office early, you know, with Mitch away.'

'Oh, Heidi, it'll be just like old times, when we had the house full of your father's business guests.'

That was true enough, Heidi thought, except that people who were paying for service often had higher expectations than ordinary house guests did. Besides, neither Geneva nor Kate was as young as when George Cameron had last filled Lilac Hill with the biggest buyers of his boxes.

But it would be cruel to point that out. And as long as Geneva thought she could handle it, the income would be awfully nice. It was only a week—they'd manage somehow. Perhaps they could hire some extra help...

'I told him that of course the meals would be extra, and I'd talk to you about working out a price for that,' Geneva went on happily. 'And I gave him a copy of our brochure, so his friends can choose the rooms they'd like.'

Heidi closed her eyes in pain. How had she managed to forget about that brochure? It not only pictured the guest rooms but listed the standard charges for each one as well—including the oriole suite, the one Dillon was occupying...

'You know, Heidi, I think we should put copies of that brochure in all the rooms instead of just mailing it out to prospective customers. Our guests could take it with them and pass it on to friends. Dillon hadn't seen it before, and he was quite interested.'

No doubt, Heidi thought. He was probably planning to file suit against her for fraud tomorrow morning.

Unless he had some other sort of deal in mind.

'I told Dillon we'd show our gratitude by adjusting his own bill,' Geneva went on. 'And do you know what he said?'

Heidi shook her head numbly.

'He said he wanted nothing but the satisfaction of making his friends happy—the old ones and the new ones too. That's just the way he said it, Heidi.'

'He's no particular friend of mine,' Heidi muttered.

Her mother didn't seem to hear. 'I had no idea what to expect when he came. From some of the things George said about his business instincts... But oh, darling, isn't Dillon the sweetest man?'

And the most lecherous, conniving, manipulative... No, perhaps that wasn't fair. He might have maneuvered Heidi into the tool-room this afternoon, but he hadn't exactly forced her into kissing him. And she had only a nasty suspicion that he might try to trade on what, after all, had been her own colossal misjudgement in overpricing his room.

Still, she couldn't bear to have her mother idolizing him, either. 'Don't forget who he is,' Heidi warned.

Geneva sighed. 'I know, but that's all in the past, Heidi. Even your father didn't seem to hold any bitterness at the end. Perhaps it's time——'

'To forget it? Sorry, Mother, but it's not past as long as the Works is struggling, and Lilac Hill takes paying guests, and Daddy's dead. Dillon Archer did that, and I'm not about to try to forget it.'

'He didn't kill George, darling.'

'And what do you think caused the heart attack? Oh, Mother——' She saw Geneva's chin start to tremble, and caught her close. 'I'm sorry. I didn't mean to upset you. You've been such a rock through this whole mess. I just don't want to see you get hurt again.'

Geneva didn't answer. But then, Heidi thought, there really wasn't anything to say.

When Heidi came into the dining-room the next morning, the garrulous Mrs Johnson was already nibbling a croissant. Across the table from her, Dillon was pouring syrup on the last bit of his waffle and listening with every appearance of interest. Geneva was at the head of the table, refilling coffee-cups and prompting the conversation now and then.

Heidi took a couple of slices of toast from the rack on the sideboard. Dillon pulled out the chair next to his for her; she considered for only a second before she took it. At least if she was sitting next to him he couldn't watch her. Besides, she'd rather not face him while she said what she needed to tell him.

Of course, she'd rather not have an audience, either— especially such an interested audience as Geneva and Mrs

Johnson would be. So Heidi leaned toward him as if to ask for the jam to be passed and said quietly, 'I need to talk to you after breakfast.'

His eyes were the strangest color, she thought. Yesterday she'd have called them gray; today they looked almost green. Or was that just a glint of satisfaction she saw?

'Let me guess what's on your mind.'

'Dillon, please. Not here.'

'You didn't sleep well last night either, and you want to know if I have any suggestions for making things better in the future?'

She pretended to ignore him.

After breakfast, Heidi dawdled around the flowerbed nearest the back door for several minutes. She had almost decided that Dillon wasn't coming at all, when he finally showed up. 'How *did* you sleep last night, Heidi?'

'Very well, thank you.'

'I'm sorry to say I didn't. Too many things on my mind, I suppose. But as long as I'm thinking about sleep...'

Color flooded her cheeks. She said through gritted teeth, 'Would you stop it?'

Dillon reached for his wallet. 'Stop what? I just meant I'd pay for tonight's stay right now, so I don't forget it later.'

She stepped back without touching the crisp bills he held out. 'Dillon, I can't take this money.'

'Why? Are you talking about the tree? I enjoyed the exercise.'

'No. It's——'

'Besides, we made a deal for that—you offered me a map of Lilac Hill. I still don't consider it a fair exchange, exactly, but——'

'You know perfectly well what I mean. I've been overcharging you.'

He smiled a little. 'Oh, that.'

Heidi waited, but he didn't seem inclined to go on. He wasn't going to make this easy, was he? 'I'll apply what you've already given me to the regular rate for that room. So you've already paid through—let's see, I think it figures out to Sunday.'

Dillon shrugged. 'I'm quite willing to continue paying the full price.'

Heidi tried to count to ten, but fury burned up good sense before she was halfway there. 'In return for what?'

His eyebrows soared. 'What are you offering? I only meant that the price seemed fair enough to me. I just assumed there was a premium for that particular room, since it used to be yours.'

'How did you know——?' Only after she'd taken the bait did Heidi realize how illogical his statement had been, and then it was too late; she'd given herself away.

Dillon was smiling. 'I didn't, actually, until just now. But there is something about it that reminds me of you— the art on the walls, and the choice of colors, perhaps. You were wearing that same unusual combination of forest-green and orange when we met.'

'That room isn't orange, it's apricot,' she said. 'And since I was wearing my Ambassadors' jacket, why you should think forest-green is a favorite color of mine——'

'Perhaps because you look so very pretty in it, with those dark brown eyes and the touch of auburn in your hair.' He held out the money. 'Take it,' he said gently. 'Or I'll give it to your mother.'

'Along with the whole story?'

'Bits and pieces of it, at least. Don't you think she'd enjoy it?'

'If you're threatening to use a simple mistake to blackmail me into sleeping with you——'

'Now, Heidi,' he chided. 'I told you I never blackmail a lady. Though I must say at the rate you're going you're proving to be less than a lady.'

She was stunned. 'Dammit, Dillon Archer, how dare you——?'

'Ladies don't tell lies. That wasn't a simple mistake, and you knew exactly what you were doing when you priced that room.' He put the money in her palm and closed her fingers over it.

Heidi gave up. She folded the cash and put it in her pocket, and watched as Dillon walked across the courtyard to his car. The sleek Jaguar roared to life and purred away down the narrow drive.

'Arguing with him is like trying to catch rainwater in a sieve,' she muttered.

And she didn't think things were likely to get better.

Mitch had left a list of companies he thought might be interested in expanding their operations to Fairview, and it took Heidi most of the day to work her way through the first third of the alphabet. If it was to do any good at all, each package had to be aimed specifically at the industry in question, detailing exactly what Fairview could offer. There was little point, for instance, in extolling the advantages of the industrial park to a retail business which would need a downtown location.

But figuring out what to emphasize was a problem which called for enormous amounts of time, thought, and research. Sometimes simply making sure the package was addressed to the proper official in each company—and that his or her name was spelled correctly—was a challenge.

She had just finished the draft of a letter and was jotting down the list of information to be included with it when she heard a man's voice in the outer office, and the secretary came to her door. 'Do you want a visitor?' she asked bluntly. 'Barry Evans says he has to see you.'

What now? Heidi thought. 'Just give me a couple of minutes, Betty, and I'll have this packet finished. Then you can let him come in.'

Heidi hadn't been alone in a room with Barry Evans since just after her father had lost the Works to Dillon, and she hadn't expected to be ever again. Nor did she particularly look forward to seeing him. One of the few good things that had come out of the whole crash, as far as Heidi was concerned, was that Barry had decided he couldn't afford to waste himself by marrying her, now that she was no longer heir to the Cameron fortune.

Not that he'd ever been crude enough to say it so plainly. He'd come to her father's funeral, and afterwards, at the cemetery, he'd talked philosophically about how unfair it was that plans could be so tangled by things outside one's own control. Heidi had known what he meant, and, since she was grateful that he wasn't going to be hanging around any more, she had held on to her temper just enough to be gracious. He might be a worm, but there was no point in stepping on him. Not even her pride was affected by his defection, and she refused to feed gossip by acting as if she'd been jilted on top of everything else.

In fact, she hadn't been rejected, for, just as Barry didn't clearly say that he'd changed his mind, he'd also never come straight out and said anything definite about spending his life with her. He'd simply acted as if the matter was all decided. He'd hung about Lilac Hill whenever Heidi came home for the weekend, treating her mother to ponderous flattery, deferring to her father, hanging on Heidi's every word, and generally behaving as if he belonged there.

That had been one of the most frustrating things about the whole affair, as far as Heidi was concerned—for as long as Barry didn't say anything definite, she couldn't squash his pretensions.

He had been so ambiguous, in fact, that for a long time she had actually tried to tell herself she was imagining things. Since Barry had worked for her father, it wasn't as if he didn't have a perfectly good reason to

visit Lilac Hill. His deference to George and his flattery
for Geneva had been easily explained by his position at
the Works. Even being nice to the boss's daughter could
be explained in that context. It didn't mean he was
necessarily attracted to Heidi.

But she'd known better. She could see it in his eyes.

Still, in the circumstances, she couldn't exactly call
him aside and tell him that she wouldn't think of marrying him even if he were the only male left in the species.
One couldn't refuse a proposal that hadn't been made!

The best she could do was to be busy whenever Barry
came, but even that hadn't discouraged him. Only the
collapse of the Works and George Cameron's death had
done that.

So what did he want now? It was business, obviously;
since her father's death Barry had called her once in a
while, and he always chatted when they met at civic
functions—but never anything which could lead to
speculation about his intentions.

Heidi buzzed the secretary and asked her to come in.
'Betty, will you type this letter up and put together the
enclosures that go with it? The list is clipped to the back
of the draft. If you can't get it out tonight, make sure
it goes in tomorrow morning's mail. And you can send
Mr Evans in.'

When Barry came in, he closed the door behind him.

This must be serious, Heidi thought. He had always
been very careful about appearances.

'I have some news,' he began.

Heidi's eyes narrowed. The Works, she thought. Barry
must still have contacts there. What had he heard that
was so serious he'd feel she needed to know?

Dillon *is* going to close it, she thought, and braced
herself against the words.

'I didn't want it to come as a shock to you,' Barry
went on, 'so I thought it best to break it to you myself.
I'm going to be married.'

Heidi had to fight down the desire to laugh in relief. If that was all . . .

Barry looked very sober. 'I hope you'll understand.'

Heidi frowned a little. She couldn't even remember seeing him with anyone in particular. Yes, she thought, Barry had always been careful. 'Congratulations, Barry.'

'I'm glad you're taking it so well.'

But Barry didn't look glad at all. He looked disappointed. For a split-second, Heidi considered throwing a fit of hysterics, simply because he so clearly expected something of the sort. But the moment of madness passed. 'I'm happy whenever any of my acquaintances has news like that. Now if there's nothing else I can do for you this afternoon, Barry . . .'

'Well, there is something I wanted to mention, as a matter of fact. The grapevine's saying that Dillon Archer's living at Lilac Hill.'

Good heavens, Heidi thought. And I believed Barry would have inside information about the Works? 'Yes, he's staying for a few days.'

Barry's jaw dropped. 'I'm surprised at you, Heidi.'

'Really?' She let a definite chill creep into her voice.

He pushed aside a stack of telephone books and sat down on the corner of her desk. 'What's going on?' he asked eagerly. 'It must be something huge. Tell me!'

What a magnificent opportunity for revenge, Heidi thought. She wouldn't have to say anything much, really. Barry would leap to conclusions, and the rumor he'd start would fly through Fairview by sunset. In fact, in one swift blow, she could not only pay Barry back for all the ridiculous assumptions he'd made over the years but strike a blow at Dillon as well. If she could just think of the right angle to embarrass *him* . . .

She let the moment pass. Stunts like that were satisfying to think about, but they almost never worked out the way they'd been intended.

She shrugged. 'He needed a place to stay. I'm running a business, after all, and money's money.'

'And that's all?' Barry was crestfallen.

'I don't know what else you expected.'

Callie's teasing words came floating out from somewhere in the back of Heidi's brain. 'Maybe he just came to get the pieces of the Cameron empire he missed last time around,' she'd said. 'There's Lilac Hill... And there's you.'

Now that rumor, Heidi thought, would be fun to start. It would rock Fairview to its foundation, that was sure.

But as for Dillon... he'd probably just laugh.

The garrulous Mrs Johnson moved out on Friday, but Lilac Hill was almost full; summer weekends were one of their busiest times.

Heidi intended to be up at first light. Instead, she overslept on Saturday morning and got downstairs just as Kate was refilling the breakfast buffet for the latecomers.

'I'm sorry,' Heidi gasped. 'My alarm didn't go off. Why didn't you buzz me on the intercom?'

'Because you needed your sleep,' Kate said brusquely. 'That's also why your alarm didn't go off.'

'You sabotaged it?'

'Your mother did. You've been working too hard.'

'So have both of you.'

'This is nothing. I've got it all under control. But I'll need all the help I can get this afternoon doing up rooms. So why don't you take it easy this morning?'

'I do have a headache,' Heidi admitted.

'Fresh air will help that. Toss a couple of croissants in a bag and go for a walk.'

It wasn't a bad idea, Heidi thought. She hadn't made her regular tour of the acreage in days. If the apple tree had blown down in that storm the other night, other things could have been damaged as well.

A couple of their guests were already strolling through the gardens; Heidi chatted for a few minutes and then walked on toward the lake. The path lay in an easy slope, twisting in and out among the old oak and maple trees.

No wonder this was her mother's favorite walk. It was beautiful in all seasons, but particularly intriguing in summer, when the leaves limited the view. As a result, each turn of the path showed a new and more beautiful vista.

The lake itself was placid, mirror-bright under the mid-morning sun. It was big enough for canoes and pedal-powered pontoons and small boats with outboard motors, but not the cabin cruiser her father had coveted. Heidi was glad; motorboats were noisy, and big ones were too elaborate to be fun. What was the point of being on the lake in the first place if one wanted all the comforts of home? It was like taking a dishwasher and a microwave on a camping trip.

She approached the water slowly, on the look-out for wildlife. The deer came at all hours of the day, and she had often seen racoons here at dusk, washing their food.

Dillon was sitting so still that she didn't see him at first, but she couldn't deny the tensing in her stomach muscles that told her he was somewhere close at hand. That reaction seemed to have gotten even stronger as the days went by. Heidi had started to wonder if the man produced some extra hormone that accounted for that phenomenon. If so, only she seemed to be able to sense it; last night he'd startled Geneva by coming up behind her.

She spotted him finally, sitting on a flat boulder at the edge of the water. He was so perfectly placed that he looked like an artist's model in the foreground of a painted landscape, looking out across the water with his elbow leaning on his knee. But there was nothing studied about the pose; he'd obviously simply sat down and made himself comfortable. She'd never seen a man before who possessed such natural grace, and for an instant she found herself wishing she'd tucked her camera in her pocket. Though what she thought she'd do with a photo of Dillon was beyond her.

Heidi considered turning back and taking another path, but he'd heard her and raised a hand. He didn't look back toward her, however, and she realized the gesture was half-greeting, half-warning.

Heidi followed his gaze across the water to the far bank. All she could see was some grass wavering as if something had recently passed through.

She could hardly avoid him; there was only the one path, and the lake was the only destination. To turn around and go back, now that he'd seen her, would make it painfully clear that she wanted to dodge him—and she suspected he'd make up for it later on. She might as well bite the bullet now.

As a matter of fact, he hadn't said anything off-color in a couple of days, so there was really no reason for her to avoid him, anyway.

Dillon started to stand up as she came up to the rock; Heidi waved him back to his comfortable position and perched on the edge with her feet drawn up.

'I was watching wild turkeys,' he said. 'A couple of adults and a whole clutch of little ones. You startled them.'

'They're pretty alert. I'm amazed they'd come out with you sitting here.'

Dillon shrugged. 'I'm a non-threatening sort.'

To a turkey, maybe, she almost said, and then thought better of it.

'This place is incredible,' he said softly. 'All of this, right in town.'

'Well, we're hardly in the middle of things. We're inside the city limits, of course, but only because my grandfather asked to be annexed. He thought it was unfair to live outside the city that produced his income and not pay his share of taxes to support it.'

'A civic-minded gentleman. That seems to run in the family.'

Heidi refused to take offense. 'True. My father was one, too... Look there! Did you see the bluebird?'

Dillon shook his head.

'They're just a flash of blue—something like a meteor streaking by.'

'That explains it. I'm hopeless at spotting meteors, too.'

'Oh, it's impossible in the city. Out here, though, it's really fairly easy.' Heidi shot a look at him. He would no doubt try to twist her simple statement into an invitation.

But he didn't. 'Perhaps you should offer special star-gazing weekends.'

'I'll consider it, if business starts to fall off. As things are going... Will you still be here next week?'

His eyebrows rose a fraction. 'Why? Would you miss me if I left?'

'I'm asking only because last night I was trying to schedule room assignments for next week. I've got a reservation for the cardinal suite for three nights and for the doves' nest for five...'

'The doves' nest? Surely you're joking.'

'I told you all the rooms are named for birds.'

'I remember. But why a nest?'

Heidi could feel the color rising in her cheeks. 'It's the master suite and very popular with honeymooners.'

'Oh. In that case,' Dillon murmured, 'why didn't you go all the way and call it the lovebirds' retreat?'

Heidi decided to ignore him. 'And then there's your pack of friends who'll need rooms all next week... Sorry, I didn't mean that the way it sounded. It's just that you've no idea what a challenge it is to make sure I have a room for everyone and that no one has to move in the middle of their stay.'

'So why do you do it? Why the bed-and-breakfast?'

'You asked that once already.' Heidi dismissed the question with a wave of her hand.

'And I didn't really get an answer, so I'm asking again. I'm surprised you're running any business at all—except maybe a book bindery. Instead, here you are operating a bed-and-breakfast and holding down a job too.'

'Use your imagination,' she said drily. 'There's not a lot of money in book-binding, and property taxes are a whole lot higher than they used to be.' She wrapped her arms around her knees. If she kept it light, perhaps he'd let the subject drop.

'You could sell the house.'

She stared at him in disbelief. His voice had been flat, unemotional—but then what else had she expected from a man capable of running a competitor's business into the ground without compunction? He wouldn't understand the sentimental attachment she had to Lilac Hill, much less the love Geneva felt for it.

Only the sounds of the wild broke the silence—the gentle lap of the water, the rustle of leaves as a breeze wandered through, the never-tiring ripple of a bird's song.

She reminded herself that bringing up all that would only encourage him to wonder about their decisions, and their finances.

'Sell it to whom?' Heidi said finally. 'A city this size doesn't have a big market for enormous houses. There are probably people who would buy it if the price was right, but Lilac Hill's worth a lot more than we could get for it. By the time we'd bought another house, there wouldn't be much left anyway. So why not keep our home? We looked at our choices and decided to let Lilac Hill pay its own way—so we have our home and the lifestyle my mother was raised to expect. If we work a little harder pleasing customers than we did taking care of ordinary guests... well, it's not that much different, really.'

He looked dissatisfied, and Heidi was relieved when he seemed to accept the way she'd glossed over the financial aspects and said, 'And that lifestyle is important to you.'

It wasn't really a question, but Heidi answered it anyway. 'It's important to her. My mother was born in that house. So was her father. Her grandfather built it. If you think for one minute we'd give it up...' She heard her voice rising with a tinge of combativeness and decided to stop before she got carried away and said too much. She slid off the rock. 'If you'll excuse me, Kate probably needs my help by now.'

Dillon didn't answer.

Just before the path twisted and the trees cut off her view, Heidi looked back over her shoulder, as casually as she could. But her caution wasn't necessary; Dillon wasn't watching her. He was staring out at the lake once more, and the landscape was once more as still as if it had been painted.

CHAPTER FIVE

'YOU'RE preoccupied today, Heidi,' Geneva said as she snapped a fresh sheet over a bed in the wren room—so called because it was the smallest of their eight guest rooms. 'I've said a half-dozen things in the last half-hour, and I don't think you've heard one of them.'

Heidi gave a last wipe to the mirror over the antique dressing-table and put her supplies back in the cleaning basket. 'Sorry, Mom. Just thinking, I guess.' She caught the opposite side of the sheet and pulled it taut.

Usually Kate took care of the day-to-day cleaning of the rooms which were in use, and after a guest's stay was finished Heidi helped with the really heavy work—scrubbing and disinfecting and turning mattresses before the next visitors arrived. But when Lilac Hill was booked full, it took all three of them just to keep up with the basics. Making beds, cleaning baths, putting out fresh towels and doing all the resulting laundry for eight rooms was a big job, especially when they had to work around their guests' schedules.

When the bed-and-breakfast had first opened, each of them had worked separately, splitting the rooms as evenly as possible. But after their first booked-full day, Heidi had taken one look at her mother's tired face and drooping shoulders and promptly suggested that the two of them form a team. They could still do as many rooms, she'd pointed out, but together they could work faster, which was less disruptive for the guest.

Her reasoning had been nothing more than an excuse, but Geneva hadn't questioned it. And so far it had worked out well; Heidi had been able discreetly to take over the physically demanding tasks in each room without ever suggesting that Geneva might not be up to the work.

But this couldn't go on, Heidi thought. For one thing, her work for the Ambassadors was taking more of her time than she'd expected; with Mitch travelling for weeks at a stretch, her job was turning out to be more than the part-time employment she'd been promised. And if Lilac Hill's bookings kept creeping up, they'd need more help. The worst part was, she couldn't promise steady employment, for the bed-and-breakfast business tended to swing from feast to famine. But perhaps Kate might know of someone who wanted work now and then...

'Heidi Jo,' Geneva said, 'do you suppose this room would look better if you put the comforter on right side up instead of the way you've got it?'

Heidi looked down at the bed. Sure enough, she'd tossed the puffy handmade quilt on upside-down. She flipped it over.

Geneva helped pull it into place. 'Are you tired, darling?'

'No more than usual. Why?'

'I heard you rustling around in the playroom last night long after I'd gone to bed.'

'There was a huge pile of bills this week.'

Geneva's brows drew together.

'I don't mean we're any worse off financially than usual,' Heidi added. 'There was just a lot more paperwork. Then I tried to schedule who gets which room next week, but that's a good deal tougher than seating the average dinner party.'

'It's a lot of work, isn't it?' Geneva arranged the throw pillows neatly on the quilt and stood back, running a professional eye over the room to check the details.

Heidi picked up the cleaning basket and the small bag of trash and led the way down the hall to her old room—

Dillon's now, for the time being at least. She'd deliberately left it till last.

She wondered how long he'd be staying. He hadn't answered that question this morning down by the lake. Come to think of it, he hadn't given her the usual wad of cash either. Was he planning to leave today?

But though the room was neat it showed the unmistakable signs of continued occupancy—shirts hung neatly in the closet, a small shaving kit in the bathroom, a briefcase full of official-looking documents on the desk, a book on the bedside table...

Her book, Heidi realized—or, rather, one of the many she'd bound for her father's library. She recognized it as an old history of Fairview which she'd bought at a flea market for a dollar, years ago. The pages had been brittle, the stitching broken, and the cover missing altogether. The rebinding she'd done was an early and amateurish job in Heidi's opinion, but George Cameron had been tickled by the supple red leather covers and the gilt title on the spine. She wondered what Dillon thought, and then reminded herself that she didn't care.

'What a thoughtful man,' Geneva said. 'He's made his bed every day he's been here, Kate tells me.'

'I don't know why you'd be impressed. It just ends up making more work when we have to tear it apart again.' Heidi started to strip the bed. Dillon had tucked the blanket in so tautly that she had to tug to get it loose.

'Don't you, dear? You see, to me it says that he feels truly like a guest here, not a paying customer.'

'And thoughtful house guests always make their beds. Well, no one's ever questioned Dillon's manners. Just his ethics.' And maybe his morals, Heidi thought, but she wasn't about to start that discussion with her mother.

Geneva dusted the tall pillars of the canopy bed and helped put on fresh sheets. 'I wonder where he grew up?' she said, almost to herself.

Heidi straightened the satin bedspread and plumped the apricot velvet cushions on the forest-green *chaise-longue* by the fireplace. It had been one of her favorite places to sit and dream, and apparently, from the way the cushions were crushed, Dillon had discovered it as well.

Sometimes, she thought, I really miss this room. And her comfortable bed, the wide window-seat where she could look out over the whole back half of the estate, the fireplace... And, of course, she missed the lifestyle those things had represented. She'd had time for reflection, time to roam Lilac Hill's paths, time to ride her mother's horses, time to play with bookbinding and crafts...

She remembered what Geneva had said just a few minutes ago about the work involved in keeping Lilac Hill open to guests. Had her mother merely been sympathetic to Heidi's difficult schedule, or was she really hinting about her own feelings? Geneva was looking tired these days too.

Heidi thought sometimes that her mother had the toughest assignment of them all. Kate could retreat to her kitchen, Heidi to her other job, but Geneva was always on public display as she dealt with their guests. She was always the gracious hostess—offering help, giving directions, assisting her guests to have a good time. Always smiling, no matter how bored she might be with their company. She did it with such tremendous charm that even Heidi didn't notice the strain—but she knew Geneva must feel it at times.

Did Geneva think fondly of a small house somewhere, vine-covered and peaceful and entirely her own? It's funny, Heidi thought, that I never considered that possibility before.

'Did I push you into this, Mother?' she said abruptly.

Geneva flicked her duster over the crystal bird sculpture on the mantel. 'What are you talking about, Heidi?'

'Would you rather have had a small house somewhere? Instead of all the trouble of the business, I mean. You're working so hard.'

Geneva's brow wrinkled.

'You know, it isn't too late to back out of this,' Heidi went on. 'We could close the bed-and-breakfast, put the house up for sale...' Despite her best intentions, there was a catch in her voice.

'Do you want to?' Geneva said quietly.

'We aren't talking about me. If you're tired of it——'

'Lilac Hill's my home, Heidi. There's no place else I'd rather be.'

Heidi relaxed. The idea of Geneva without Lilac Hill— or, for that matter, Lilac Hill without Geneva—was unthinkable, and yet... It was because of Dillon that the idea had even occurred to her, she realized. He'd mentioned the possibility of selling the house, and the suggestion had been simmering in her subconscious ever since. The man was a troublemaker, that was all.

She started for the hall to get the vacuum cleaner and for the first time saw that the picture over the mantel wasn't the same as the last time she'd been in here. The Audubon print of a pair of Baltimore orioles was gone, and in its place was an oval frame with an oil portrait of a child.

'Where did my Audubon print go?' she asked. 'And why is my baby picture hanging in its place?'

'I forgot to tell you that last week when I took the print down to clean the frame I dropped it and broke the glass. Rather than leave a blank spot, I brought this downstairs. Don't you think it looks good there? You were such a pretty child, with those big brown eyes and the dark curls.'

'And the chubby cheeks,' Heidi sighed. No wonder Dillon had made that crack about the art in this room reminding him of her. From his point of view, it must have been a dead giveaway.

On Sunday mornings their guests usually wanted breakfast later than during the week, but when Heidi came downstairs laughter was already floating from the dining-room. At least everyone seemed to be in a good mood, she thought. That must mean Kate was keeping up with the breakfast rush. Still, why hadn't the woman called her down to help?

How long could Kate keep up this pace, anyway? They really must hire someone soon. Not that Kate would take easily to sharing her kitchen, but perhaps if Heidi could find someone she liked...

'Good morning.' Dillon rose from a chair in a dim corner of the great hall and came toward the foot of the stairs. 'Oh, good, you're wearing walking shoes.'

'Why should it matter?'

'Because I wouldn't want to carry you all the way back if you sprained an ankle. Come along.'

Heidi looked at him as if he'd lost his mind. 'All the way back from where? What do you think you're doing?'

'Isn't it obvious? I'm kidnapping you.'

She decided to humor him. 'That's lovely, Dillon, but I'm afraid you can't kidnap me without Kate's permission. She needs me to help with breakfast. So you go negotiate with her and I'll——'

'I already have, and she says she doesn't need you because she's got it under control. You see, I told her that you promised me a map of the paths around Lilac Hill and didn't produce it.'

'I forgot. I've had a whole lot of other things to do the last few days.'

'I don't doubt it. Nevertheless, Kate agrees with me that promises to guests are very important and must be given top priority.'

Heidi looked up at him in exasperation. What was the big deal, anyway? And why did he even want a map? Half the fun of exploring was not knowing where one would end up. But she supposed there wasn't any point in trying to explain that to him. 'All right. I'll go draw the map right now.'

Dillon shook his head. 'Yesterday that would have been good enough to satisfy me, but not today. In the time it will take to sketch any kind of map, we could walk halfway round the property. And since this is my last chance to see it...'

His last chance? He was leaving today, then?

Heidi felt a tinge of sadness ripple through her body. I'll miss him, she thought, and caught herself up short. Sure she'd miss him—just the same way she mourned a summer head cold when it finally went away! She'd miss the money, of course; maybe she shouldn't go ahead with the tennis court project just yet.

'In fact, Kate even packed breakfast for us.' He waved a hand toward the chair where he'd been sitting. Sure enough, there was a knapsack on the floor. 'Shall we go?'

Heidi admitted, 'I'd like to know how you managed to get a picnic out of Kate at this hour of the morning.'

'Sheer charm,' he said modestly. 'And playing on her sympathy. She thinks with the amount I'm paying for my room I deserve some personal attention and entertainment.'

'You *told* her how much you're paying?' Heidi's voice was just short of a shriek.

'Oh, no. Her opinion was based on your regular rates. If I told her what you're really charging me, she'd probably wrap you up and deliver you to my door as a virgin sacrifice.' He eyed her with interest. 'Now that I come to think of it, perhaps I should have another short talk with Kate. If you'll wait right here...'

Heidi capitulated. After all, the man was leaving. A couple more hours in his company wouldn't hurt her. 'The tour leaves this moment or not at all. Are you coming along?'

'Certainly I am.' He slung the knapsack over his shoulder and held the back door open for her. 'As long as we're talking about it, though, you've roused my curiosity. If Kate would happen to deliver you to my door——'

'Dillon, if you don't mind——'

'*Would* you be a virgin sacrifice?'

Heidi stopped in the courtyard. 'That does it.'

'I was just asking,' Dillon pointed out. 'I suppose I could quiz Kate instead, but——'

'If you make any more suggestive remarks, I'll strand you at the far corner of the property and make you find your own way back. Got it?'

'Yes, ma'am,' he said meekly. 'Which way, my lovely guide?'

Heidi shot a look at him.

'That's not suggestive,' Dillon argued. 'That's simple fact.'

Heidi decided it wasn't worth arguing about; if he thought that sort of remark would get to her, he'd never quit. 'Toward the lake, but we'll branch off before we get to the water.'

'I didn't see any other path yesterday when I came this way.'

'Do you expect signposts? It's a deer trail, for heaven's sake, not a freeway. Where did you grow up, anyway?'

'South Chicago. In our neighborhood, we didn't spend much time thinking about deer trails. In fact, any enterprising blade of grass that stuck its head up more than two inches was apt to be used as home plate in a baseball game.'

The idea of a childhood spent without constant contact with nature made Heidi feel faintly horrified. But Dillon sounded quite calm about it.

She said, 'I suppose that means you don't know your trees either.'

'Of course I do.' He pointed. 'That's a tree, and...'

Heidi spent the next fifteen minutes pointing out the differences between birches and oaks and maples and mulberries, and she led the way down an even harder-to-see path to a little glade full of dogwoods. 'See how the leaves and branches seem to float?' she said, and Dillon nodded as if he was absorbing every word. 'They're especially beautiful when they bloom white in the spring.'

The path was steep and so narrow that they had to go single file. Heidi climbed out of the little glade first, terribly aware that Dillon was right behind her.

'Nice view,' he said, and she wheeled around to face him. 'Of the dogwoods,' he added, and smiled. 'What did you think I meant, Heidi?'

They were very nearly at the furthest extent of Lilac Hill when Heidi said, 'Should we see what Kate put in that knapsack?'

'I thought you'd forgotten it.' Dillon looked around. 'This isn't exactly the picnic spot I'd have chosen, but obviously you know best.'

'It's not my choice either. It's too dark and cool under all these trees. Wait just a minute.'

The path turned a few feet ahead of them and opened out into a natural little clearing carpeted with prairie grass and wild flowers. A tiny stream ran through the center of the open area, murmuring to itself as it rippled over the stones in its path.

Heidi knelt in a sunny spot on the stream's bank and held out a hand for the knapsack. Dillon gave it to her and remained standing, hands in the pockets of his khaki trousers, looking around.

'This is one of my favorite spots on the whole estate,' Heidi said. 'No, it's more than that—it's one of the best places in the world as far as I'm concerned. I used to bring a book out here on summer days and lie on that branch and read.' She pointed to a great oak at the edge of the clearing. One gigantic horizontal limb stretched almost to the creek.

Dillon judged the distance up from the ground and the lack of other branches to serve as rungs. 'You were quite a tree-climber, weren't you?'

Heidi nodded. 'It wasn't just trees, though. I climbed the shelves in the library before I could walk, and I absolutely adored upright pianos—they're very easy to get on top of, you know. Mother says it's why she has white hair. Can you imagine Lilac Hill with child-proof gates at the top and bottom of every staircase?'

Dillon shook his head.

'There are pictures in my baby book. The gates had to be specially made, too, because the steps are so wide.'

He smiled. 'I'm surprised they didn't just lock you in your nursery till you grew up.'

'Daddy said I'd probably have found a way out the window and on to the roof.' She sobered abruptly. For a moment there, she'd forgotten whom she was talking to. It was one thing to talk about herself, something else to share those precious memories of her father with a man who had indirectly hastened his death. 'I wonder what Kate packed for us?' she added coolly.

Dillon sat down beside her, folding his long legs. 'Was it a lonely childhood?'

'From the perspective of a constant baseball game, I'm sure it seems that way.'

'Well—yes, a bit.'

'There were other kids near by if I wanted them. I just didn't want them much.'

She spread a large tea-towel out on the grass and arranged the food on it. There were big chunks of ham and cheese and half a dozen of Kate's light-as-a-feather biscuits, still slightly warm, with her own combination of honey and butter in a squeeze bottle. There was also a generous bag of red grapes and a Thermos of coffee. Heidi poured two cups full and sliced some of the ham and cheese into bite-sized pieces.

'Now this is heaven,' Dillon said, cradling his cup in one hand. 'I wonder how I rated this? All I asked Kate for was a couple of peanut butter sandwiches and some apples.'

Heidi, who'd been wondering the same thing, nodded. 'That explains it. Kate doesn't consider peanut butter to be food.' She split a biscuit, drizzled the honey and butter combination over both pieces, and held one half out to him. 'Try this. It's positively one of the best taste sensations ever.'

Dillon didn't take the biscuit. Instead his fingers closed gently around Heidi's wrist. As he bent his head to take a bite, his breath tickled her palm. His touch seemed to heat her blood, and her heart was pounding. She hoped he couldn't feel the pulse in her wrist.

She looked down at him, noting the elegant shape of his ear and the way his dark hair curled slightly at the ends. Her fingertips tingled with the desire to trace the line of his ear, to smooth the curls into place.

I wish things were different, she thought. I wish he weren't who he is. I wish at least I didn't know his name. If I didn't know who he was——

She caught herself up short. It was mad to think she could care about Dillon. Whether she knew his name or not didn't make a difference to the sort of person he was. And though he might not have directly showed her the ruthless side of him, it was plain he was a man who went after what he wanted and usually got it—regardless of the consequences to others. That quality had been obvious even before she'd known who he was. And since it was that characteristic of his which had ruined George Cameron's business...

Her mother had said it was all over and it was time to forget it. But it wasn't past; Geneva was wrong.

Dillon finished the biscuit and slowly released her wrist. Heidi's heart-rate slowed gradually, but her fingers still trembled slightly as she reached for a bit of ham. 'Are you going to close the Works, Dillon?'

He frowned. 'Why would you think that?'

'That's what some of the employees believe. It makes sense—you haven't done a thing to improve the facilities, and you haven't replaced a single worker who's quit or retired in the last year.'

'Haven't needed the manpower.'

'I don't expect you have,' she agreed. 'I understand sales are way down, too.'

He reached for a chunk of cheese. 'You seem to know a lot about my business.'

'I do have an interest in the subject. Besides, there must be a reason for your being here.'

'Do you always show such fascination with your guests' affairs?'

She said thoughtfully, 'You can't have it both ways, Dillon.'

'I'm not sure what you mean.'

'You can't behave like an invited guest and also be simply a paying customer who treats Lilac Hill like a hotel and expects Mother and me not to show a speck of interest in the Works.'

'That sounds like a marvelous excuse for nosiness.'

'It's not prying to ask a simple question. And you've invited interest by acting as if you're a friend of the family. If you'd decided to stay at the hotel, would you be taking the assistant manager out for a walk and for breakfast this morning—whether she wanted to go or not? I don't think so.'

His smile flashed. 'Oh, that depends. Is she a lot like you?'

Heidi gave him a level look. 'You're not going to answer me, are you?'

He reached for another biscuit. 'I can't.'

Heidi was puzzled. 'What do you mean, you can't? It's not some classified secret—it will come out sooner or later.'

'I mean I don't know.' He smiled at her as he layered cheese and ham on his biscuit.

Heidi was startled. He didn't *know* whether he was going to close the Works or not? That made no sense whatever, for if there was one thing Dillon wasn't it was indecisive.

'That's incredible. I'd bet you can make that analysis with one look at the bottom line of the plant's balance sheet.'

'If I could, I wouldn't be here looking it over in person. Nevertheless, thank you for your high opinion of my financial acumen.' He finished eating his biscuit, lay back against the soft grass with his head propped against a fallen log and his coffee-cup perched on his chest, and closed his eyes. He looked comfortable enough to stay there all day.

Heidi gave up. If she built a fire and held his toes to the flame, he might talk, but nothing short of that was likely to get her any answers. She might as well save her dignity, and at any rate she had her answer—he hadn't denied that he was thinking of closing the Works.

She started to gather up the remains of their picnic and repack the knapsack.

Dillon's breathing deepened as he slid further into sleep. Heidi half expected him to start snoring at any moment, or at least to take a breath deep enough to upset his coffee-cup and spill the still warm liquid all over him. For a moment, she enjoyed picturing the resulting scene, then reluctantly reached for the cup. It might be fun to watch, but it wasn't very sporting.

She leaned over and eased the cup off his chest. She was being so careful not to wake him that when his hand abruptly closed like iron around her wrist she was so startled that she dropped the cup. Droplets of lukewarm coffee flew everywhere, splattering both of them.

'Now see what you've done!' Heidi brushed futilely at the wet brown dots on the front of her blouse.

'I didn't do anything,' Dillon said. 'That cup was perfectly safe till you interfered.' He pulled, ever so gently.

Heidi was already off balance, and with one hand trapped in his grip she couldn't save herself from tumbling. She ended up sprawled across him with one arm outflung, her fingers braced against the grass in an attempt to hold herself aloof. Both Dillon's hands rested on the small of her back, and slowly he exerted pressure, pulling her down toward him.

'You promised,' she managed to say.

'I seem to remember agreeing to make no suggestive remarks.' His voice was husky. 'But I don't recall anybody saying a thing about kisses.'

She was watching his eyes, fascinated despite herself by the fact that they had grown ever darker. There was no mischievous light in them, just something unfathomable and disturbingly warm.

It wouldn't be very effective to struggle, she thought. She couldn't possibly get enough leverage to free herself, and fighting him might only pique his interest more. Besides, if all he wanted was a kiss—and he couldn't possibly have anything more in mind, out here in the open like this—what harm could it do to kiss him? In other circumstances, she could have liked this man.

She was vaguely aware that there was something wrong with that logic, but she had neither time nor wisdom enough to figure out the flaw, for, as if he had felt the resistance go out of her, Dillon's hand slid up her spine and cupped the back of her head, urging her down to meet his lips.

The embrace went on till Heidi couldn't remember a time when she hadn't been kissing him, hadn't been held securely in his arms. Even after he stopped kissing her and only held her gently, she snuggled against him, enjoying the warmth of his body and the way his breathing rocked her.

'Well.' The way he said it made the word about three syllables long. 'You do pack a punch, don't you? Now that we've got that bit of fiction out of the way——'

'Fiction?' Heidi's voice sounded a little fuzzy to her own ears. 'What do you mean?'

Dillon's fingers slid through her hair, capturing the glossy mass of it at the back of her neck. 'The idea that you can't stand me. Now the question is whether this little spot is quite private enough to finish what we've started. On the whole, I'm inclined to think it is, but——'

Heidi braced both hands on his chest and lunged free. Dillon gave a little grunt of pain at the sudden pressure, and his fingers caught in her hair as she pulled away. She felt for an instant as if her scalp was being ripped off, and tears rose to her eyes.

'No?' Dillon said. He sat up lazily. 'Well, you're the expert, I suppose.'

'It's got nothing to do with privacy. If this were the Garden of Eden and we were the only two people in it——'

Dillon finished the sentence for her. 'I know, you wouldn't make love with me. At least that's what you say. But just what do you think you were doing a couple of minutes ago, anyway?'

Her face was burning. 'That was only a kiss.'

'*Only* a kiss? Oh, my dear Heidi...'

'Let's get one thing straight, Dillon. You're not bad-looking, and you've got a certain talent when it comes to kissing, but——'

'Thank you.'

'But nothing changes the facts. I'm not about to forget the fact that you drove my father's business to the wall, and then bought what was left of it for a pittance.'

'I paid what it was worth, Heidi.'

'And why was it worth so little? Because you'd already stolen his customers.'

Dillon was on his feet. 'Now wait just a minute. I didn't steal anything, Heidi. That was normal business competition.'

'You can play with words all you want, Dillon, but the fact is you cheated him and drove him to the brink of bankruptcy.'

The words rang in the little clearing, and for a long time the accusation seemed to echo.

Dillon's face was hard, his eyes shuttered as if he was seeing things he didn't want to look at. Things like his own responsibility for what had happened to George Cameron, Heidi thought. Well, maybe it was time he took a good long look at that.

She knelt to gather up the remains of their picnic. She retrieved Dillon's cast-aside cup and shook out the few remaining drops of coffee.

'And that's why Lilac Hill is a bed-and-breakfast.' His voice was quiet, but it held a hard undertone. 'Because you're broke. I admit I've been a little slow. Just how long have you blamed me for what happened to the Works?'

Heidi said, as if she were explaining to a child, 'Since you caused it—when you started slashing your prices and taking his customers.'

'I told you what I did was normal business competition.'

'Then I'm glad I'm not competing with you.' She zipped the knapsack and slung it over her shoulder. 'I'm sorry your tour of Lilac Hill didn't turn out very well. I hope you'll remember your stay with good feelings——'

'And not discourage my friends from coming tomorrow? What a cold-hearted little promoter you are!' He reached for her; Heidi tried to side-step him and tripped over a fallen branch. She caught herself awkwardly.

Dillon waited till she was steady and then held out his hand once more. 'If you'll allow me,' he said with cool politeness. 'I was offering to carry the knapsack.'

She handed it over and plunged down the path which led most directly to Lilac Hill. She didn't look over her shoulder to see if he was following.

It seemed to Heidi that the paths had never been so steep nor the air so thick and gloomy and hard to breathe. She was furious with herself, even more angry than she was with him. He'd been out of line, of course, kissing her like that and then implying that she was as eager to make love as he obviously was. But she'd been in the wrong, too, lashing out at him as she had. No matter how he behaved, he was still a guest, and one didn't treat a guest that way.

At the last turning before the path's end, she paused so abruptly that Dillon collided with her before he could stop. 'What the hell . . . ?' he said.

She took two careful steps out of his way and turned to face him. She couldn't look directly at him, so she chose a stripe in the collar of his shirt and tried not to remember how she'd nuzzled her face against that very stripe a few minutes ago. 'I shouldn't have said all that.'

'What a gracious apology.'

Heidi bit her lip and ignored the edge in his voice. 'Mother's right about one thing—it's all past, and nothing will change it now, so it was pointless to pop off at you. Even if you did need to hear some home truths. But I don't know what good I expected it to do.' She shrugged. 'Anyway, I really am sorry to have your stay end this way.'

His mouth curved a little, but only a satirist would have called it a smile. 'But Heidi,' he said quietly, 'who ever said I was leaving?'

CHAPTER SIX

HEIDI was stunned. Of course he'd said he was leaving! He'd told her when he'd practically dragged her out of the house this morning that this would be his last chance to see the estate...

On the other hand, she abruptly recalled, he'd also said he didn't know what he was going to do with the Works. But she'd already been convinced of his intention to go away, so it hadn't occurred to her to wonder if it was logical for him to leave Fairview before that decision was made.

But why shouldn't he go away? Surely by now he'd seen all he needed to see of the Works. Analyzing his observations and making his decision could be done anywhere, couldn't it? And surely he had other things to do; after all, his business interests covered half a dozen states.

So had he really changed his mind because of her outburst?

That was a truly crazy idea, she told herself. Now that he knew precisely what she thought of him, why on earth would he want to stick around?

He didn't, of course. The only answer was that she was becoming paranoid.

Dillon stepped around her and went on toward the house. He waited punctiliously at the back door, however, and held it for her. Heidi wished he hadn't; she felt bad enough at the moment, and it would have been some small comfort if Dillon had given up the public display of manners just once.

Though why she should feel so bad about telling him the truth was beyond her. Certainly there was a code of etiquette about the way a guest should be treated, but there were limits about proper behavior toward a hostess, too, and he'd breached those first. Trying to seduce her—and very nearly succeeding...

Perhaps what was really bothering her, Heidi concluded, was having to admit how tempted she'd been, and how easily she'd forgotten her dislike of him the moment he'd started to kiss her. It was not a reaction she was proud of, and she had to admit she had no guarantee that if it ever happened again she'd react differently.

But of course it wouldn't happen again. She wouldn't allow it. Besides, Dillon wouldn't be likely to push the matter, either. After the things she'd said to him, he'd probably avoid her altogether.

She told herself that the odd feeling in her stomach was relief.

When Heidi came home from work on Monday afternoon, Geneva was crossing the front hall with a silver tray full of delicate hors d'oeuvres. Heidi eyed the titbits and said, 'Dillon's friends must be here.'

'Such nice people,' Geneva said absently. 'You'll come down and join us for a drink, won't you?'

The last thing Heidi wanted was to barge in on Dillon's party—and despite Geneva's presence Heidi was positive this was very much Dillon's party. 'Why don't you let me pretend to be the maid?' she said. 'Kate will need help serving dinner, and——'

'She's got a friend helping out tonight, so you won't even need to fuss about the dishes afterward. Besides, I need you to help entertain all these people.'

Heidi tried to smother her sigh. 'All right. I'll change and be right down.'

'You'll like them, Heidi. I do.'

Heidi didn't doubt Geneva's feelings. Her mother really enjoyed each new guest, and even when she was tired her warmth and friendliness were natural and un-forced. Heidi, on the other hand, was finding that sometimes she had to work harder at it than she'd thought possible.

The idea of a bed-and-breakfast had looked so simple when Heidi first came up with it. In her growing-up years, Lilac Hill was often full of house guests. It had been built for that purpose, and Geneva had been hap-piest when she had a crowd of people around. Whether they were friends or George Cameron's business con-tacts hadn't seemed to make a difference.

And running a bed-and-breakfast would be simple compared to the way they had entertained before. Their guests would amuse themselves for a good part of the time, without the need for pool parties and riding ex-peditions. Or, for that matter, lunches and dinners.

And it would still look like a good idea, Heidi told herself, if it weren't for Dillon Archer. So just grit your teeth and hang on, because he can't stay forever.

She surveyed her closet doubtfully. She would have liked to change into comfortable trousers and a cotton sweater and flat shoes. But the basic black cocktail dress Geneva had been wearing—simple though it was—had warned her that something more formal than her usual attire was required.

The problem was Heidi didn't have anything quite comparable. These days, her wardrobe ran to skirts which would co-ordinate with the Ambassadors' green jacket—not to party dresses.

Though who was she trying to impress? she asked herself rudely, and dragged a teal-blue dress off the hanger. It was more than a year old, but the color looked good on her, emphasizing the auburn highlights in her dark brown hair, and the style was classic.

She'd go down and have a drink and be charming to Dillon's guests—and pay no attention to Dillon himself. That shouldn't be difficult. If she was careful, even he couldn't be certain she was avoiding him; there would be plenty of other people to keep her occupied.

She couldn't quite ignore him, of course. Heidi knew the moment she walked into the library which corner of the room Dillon was in—the sensation was like a magnetic pull, and she had to exert effort to keep from looking in his direction. Instead she focused on her mother, who was talking to a white-haired couple. Geneva looked up with a smile and introduced them as Mr and Mrs Hale.

Two men jumped up from their chairs by the fireplace to be presented. They were much of an age—past forty, Heidi estimated—and they looked remarkably alike. Not only was there a certain facial resemblance, but their business suits could have been cut from the same bolt of cloth, and their attitudes were similar—the way they stood, and a certain tilt of the head.

They're sort of like Tweedledum and Tweedledee, Heidi thought, and hoped she could keep them straight.

'And Adrienne Collins,' Geneva finished, and with reluctance Heidi turned toward the corner where Dillon sat.

She wasn't surprised to see him getting up from the arm of a big leather-covered wing-backed chair. And she wasn't surprised to see that the woman sitting in the chair was a certified beauty. Adrienne Collins' eyes were emerald-green and slanted like a cat's. Her black hair was up-swept, her long jet earrings swished sensually with every movement, and her red dress had crept high, showing perfect legs, elegantly crossed.

'Miss Collins,' Heidi said. 'Welcome to Lilac Hill.'

'I prefer to be called Ms.' The woman's voice was low and a bit rough.

Of course, Heidi thought. She's divorced—or perhaps still married. Though why Heidi was wasting her time being judgemental was beyond her comprehension. Adrienne Collins' marital arrangements weren't any of her business.

She had to walk past Dillon to reach the bar. It wasn't that she wanted a drink exactly, but she needed something to hold on to. But she had taken no more than a few steps before she wished she'd settled for something else to occupy her hands. That overwhelming sense of awareness increased the nearer she came to him, till she thought she might suffocate.

No one could ever mistake Dillon for anyone else, she thought. Even before she'd known his name, she'd recognized him in a more elemental way—the man had an impact that she'd never experienced in any other person. It wasn't a matter of looks, though he was certainly attractive. It wasn't clothes, though obviously his suit hadn't come off the rack. He simply had a presence— an aura of energy—that was unlike anything she'd ever known before.

By the time she'd poured her sherry, Dillon had resumed his seat on the arm of Adrienne's chair, one elbow propped on the back of it and his head bent confidingly toward her.

But his absorption in the other woman didn't ease Heidi's overwhelming awareness of his presence. That surprised her a little, for she'd always thought Dillon had caused a good deal of that sensation on purpose. When she'd felt the impact of his presence most strongly, he'd always been watching her. Even when she'd walked into the library tonight, she'd assumed that he'd seen her entrance.

Now he was concentrating on Adrienne, but still Heidi felt that breathless ache she'd first experienced in the solarium at the Ambassadors' lunch when her eyes had first fallen on Dillon.

It'll go away when he does, she told herself, and wondered when that was likely to be. Now that his friends were encamped at Lilac Hill...

It was a strange group of friends, though, Heidi thought—except of course for Adrienne Collins, who was easily explained. A couple old enough to be Dillon's parents, and two men who didn't strike her as the type to be his best buddies...

Heidi sat down with Tweedledum and Tweedledee—what *were* their names? She knew darned well Geneva wouldn't have forgotten, or mixed them up, but then Geneva had fewer things on her mind than Heidi did.

The two men didn't seem to notice that she'd joined them. Neither rose, and Tweedledum kept right on talking about fusion bonding—whatever that was. Heidi was seriously over her head; she was ready to creep away when Tweedledee finally noticed she was there, half rose from his chair, and hushed his companion with a gesture.

'Oh, do continue,' Heidi said. 'You're so absorbed in your conversation it would be a shame to interrupt.'

'Heavens, no. We'd be rude to carry on,' Tweedledee said.

The two of them smiled at her. The silence lengthened.

Finally Heidi said desperately, 'What is fusion bonding, anyway?'

'It's an interesting development in thermoplastics.' Tweedledum sounded quite cheerful about it.

Heidi thought he might as well have been speaking Martian, though he obviously believed he was making sense. At least, he didn't offer a fuller explanation.

She was groping for another topic of conversation when Kate rang the dinner-bell. Heidi jumped up with alacrity.

'Dillon, dear, would you escort Mrs Hale into the dining-room, please?' Geneva murmured.

Heidi happened to see Adrienne's face just then, as the cat-like eyes narrowed and looked quite cold for an instant. Then with a laugh Adrienne turned toward Tweedledum and said, 'We seem to be paired off together.'

The poor man looked as terrified, Heidi thought, as if a vulture had come up to him and asked to be introduced.

In the dining-room, the subtle light of the chandelier was supplemented by candles. The linen was Geneva's best, and the crystal sparkled. Tiny china place-cards marked each setting, the names neatly written in Geneva's flowing hand.

Heidi glanced at them with satisfaction. Dinner for eight without an official host made for an awkward table, and she was glad she'd thought to check the dining-room when she'd first come downstairs to see just what arrangement Geneva had decided to use. She'd probably get a scolding from her mother later for the switch she'd made, but it would be worth it—at least she wouldn't have to suffer through an entire dinner with Dillon beside her.

She moved easily around to the foot of the table, opposite her mother. 'I think you're beside me,' she told Tweedledee.

He pulled out the chair to her right; then abruptly his hand dropped as if he'd been burned. He backed away, directly into Dillon, and said, 'Excuse me, sir.'

Sir? Heidi thought. He actually called Dillon sir? This was positively the strangest group of friends she'd ever encountered.

Dillon seated Mrs Hale and took the chair next to Heidi's. Heidi raised an eyebrow. 'I don't think you're intended to sit there,' she said under her breath. 'What's the matter, Dillon? Couldn't stay away from me?'

He didn't say a word, just turned the place-card so she could see it. 'Mr Archer', it said as clearly as could be.

Heidi blinked in disbelief. How had Geneva switched the place-cards back? She hadn't left the library since Heidi had joined the group. And neither had Dillon—not that he'd want to switch the cards, of course.

Heidi concluded that the culprit must have been Kate, straightening out what she probably thought was Geneva's careless error. Well, there was no point in getting upset about it now. Heidi could hardly complain to her mother about Kate's ruthless efficiency when she'd have to expose her own little scheme in the process.

If I just get through tonight, she thought, tomorrow I'll find an excuse to escape. Tomorrow Mother can handle dinner on her own, because she'll be old friends with all of them by then.

At least as close as they were to each other, she thought, remembering that 'sir'. It didn't sound as if they were such an intimate group of pals, after all.

And in that case, what *had* brought them all to Lilac Hill?

After dinner, she helped Geneva pour coffee in the drawing-room and then murmured an excuse and slipped out the French doors on to the terrace beyond. Darkness had not quite fallen; a lone late whippoorwill called a couple of times and then fell silent. But the evening wasn't quiet; the rhythmic creak of cicadas filled the air.

The drawing-room lights fell in long bars across the brick floor of the terrace, and she could hear the murmur of voices, and a woman's laugh. Adrienne's, perhaps? No, Heidi thought. More likely Mrs Hale's—it had been a sincere laugh.

She walked a hundred yards toward the barn and then turned back toward the house. The paths were too rough for her high-heeled shoes, and the mosquitoes were starting to bite. But she couldn't face the group in the drawing-room, either. Mrs Hale had seemed to want to talk to her, but Heidi needed to be alone.

She found the solarium door unlocked and slipped inside, pushing open a set of casement windows that overlooked the flower garden. Warm, fragrant air spilled in, and she sat down on the low marble sill to watch the moon rise.

It was full tonight, and powerful bluish light crept into the solarium, drawing ever-changing patterns of the high-arched windows on to the black and white marble floor. She wondered if her great-grandfather had sat here when Lilac Hill was new, watching the moonlight.

The drawing-room lights went off, leaving the terrace bathed only in the glow of the moon. Heidi heard Tweedledum and Tweedledee pass the solarium door—they were talking about lasers now, she noted. Mr and Mrs Hale went down the hall toward the staircase. Geneva followed them.

Dillon and Adrienne Collins didn't.

They must have gone off somewhere while she was walking outside, Heidi thought. Surely they weren't still in a dark corner of the drawing-room.

She reached out to close the casements, and from the corner of her eye she caught a flash of red from the terrace.

Adrienne had draped a fringed red shawl over her bare-shouldered dress. It was so lacy that it couldn't offer much warmth, and Heidi doubted it would be much protection from the mosquitoes, either. Beside her, Dillon was a dark shadow—though Heidi didn't need to see him clearly to know who was there. Her early-warning system was still in full operation where he was concerned.

She closed the windows, intending to go straight up to her room. She was too well-mannered to eavesdrop, and considering who was on the terrace she had no interest anyway. But as the latch snapped into place, Adrienne asked, 'What was that?'

Dillon said, 'Just a creak. Old houses do that, you know.'

Heidi frowned. She shouldn't have been able to hear them so clearly. Unless there were other windows still open—and if so, she'd better secure them in case the weather changed during the night. If the wind came up and whipped those delicate glass panels, she didn't want to think about the damage it would cause.

She started across the solarium. The windows all appeared to be closed. She was going to have to check each one.

Adrienne sat down on the low brick wall which surrounded the terrace. 'So what's the mystery, Dillon? Why did you call us all together here? You know perfectly well what we're going to say.' Her voice was low, but it carried clearly.

Heidi paused. She was probably going to hear a whole lot more of this conversation before she found the open window. And that wasn't the worst of it. The likelihood was that any minute one of them would look up and see her—though the solarium was dark, the moonlight made it unlikely that she could stay hidden. And even if she could remain out of sight, the window latch would without doubt make a noise. Then there would be no convincing anyone she hadn't deliberately listened.

'The same thing you've been saying all along,' Dillon answered.

'That's right. Closing the plant is the only thing that makes sense, and the sooner we start working out the details...'

Heidi gritted her teeth and sank down on to the floor, where she couldn't be seen.

She had suspected for days that the Works was doomed. And yet, now that the axe was falling, she realized that deep in her heart she had believed that Dillon wouldn't let it come to that. Somehow he would save it...

Foolish you, she told herself, to put so much as a shred of faith in his goodwill! How stupid to picture him as some kind of knight on a white horse riding to the rescue, when the truth is he's been the villain of the piece from the beginning.

Why should she expect him to feel commitment to Fairview? Dillon didn't owe the city anything; there hadn't even been any concessions or bonuses to persuade him to bring his business to town. And as for his workers—well, they weren't real people to Dillon, at least not the way they had been to George Cameron and to Heidi's grandfather and great-grandfather before him. They had not only known their workers but every wife's name and where the kids went to school. When George Cameron had walked through the Works, he'd had a question or a comment for almost everyone.

It was then Heidi recalled something from her most recent tour of the plant, a detail that had stuck in her memory even though she hadn't really seen it at the time. There had been too many other things on her mind that day to notice consciously that not once in the whole tour had Dillon paused to talk to a worker.

He probably doesn't want to get to know them, she thought grimly. It might make it a little harder to put them out of work if they were more than just statistics.

'I know that's the sensible choice,' Dillon said quietly. 'I just want to hear it again before I decide.'

Heidi chewed on her bottom lip, remembering how he'd said that he didn't know what he would do with the Works. Perhaps she was judging him too harshly; perhaps he honestly hadn't made up his mind. If that was so, maybe it wasn't too late. Though what kind of appeal might be able to counterbalance the kind of advice he was getting now was beyond her.

'You don't mind going over it all again, do you?' His tone was almost whimsical.

Adrienne gave a low, sultry laugh. 'Of course not, darling. The surroundings are pleasant enough, the food's decent…and convincing you is always fun, Dillon, dear.' She raised a hand to his cheek and whispered something. Her face was tilted up to his, her lips parted slightly.

Waiting to be kissed, Heidi thought. The iron band around her heart clenched just a little tighter.

Then Adrienne jerked away and slapped her arm. 'Damned bugs! I'm not going to stay out here and be eaten alive.' She smiled up at Dillon. 'You may come up to my room.'

Dillon didn't answer, just held out a hand.

Heidi waited till their quiet footsteps had passed the solarium door, and let another couple of minutes go by before she stirred. She secured the last open window, checked the French door in the drawing-room—amazingly, Dillon had remembered to lock it—and took the servants' stairs at the far end of the house rather than risk them seeing her on the landing of the main staircase.

Not that they'd be looking, she thought irritably. And probably they wouldn't be lurking in the hallway, either. They'd be securely inside Adrienne's room—the sandpiper suite—long before Heidi got to the third floor.

Not that she cared, she told herself firmly. The only thing that mattered much now was the Works. Maybe there was still a way to save it.

When Heidi came into the dining-room the next morning, Tweedledum and Tweedledee were just sitting down with coffee and Kate's puffy sweet rolls. They seemed to be discussing the hardening points of various polymers.

How do they do it? Heidi thought. It's hardly even light outside!

They cut the conversation off, however, as she took her own chair. 'Don't mind me,' she said. 'I never comprehend anything before breakfast anyway, so you might as well carry on.'

Adrienne appeared, wearing a blindingly white blouse and a tailored black suit with a short, narrow skirt which showed off her legs. It was far from being the casual sort of clothing she might wear on the vacation she was ostensibly enjoying. Contrary to Heidi's expectations, she did not look like a cat who'd just licked out the cream pitcher.

That's because she's already got her attention on business, Heidi thought, noting the leather portfolio Adrienne was carrying. That no doubt made her a woman of Dillon's own mind, didn't it? Business during business hours was his motto, he had said. And as for what happened the rest of the day—and night...

Suddenly Heidi wasn't very hungry. She cleared her place and stacked her dishes on the cart by the door to the butler's pantry.

In the hallway, Dillon was leaning against the newel post at the foot of the stairs, looking up at Geneva, who stood three steps up.

'You could use the music-room,' Geneva said. 'The furniture's not terribly comfortable, you understand. That's why we don't use it much. But it's private.'

'That will do. Also, do you have a blackboard or something of the sort?'

'A blackboard?' Heidi said. 'Funny, this group didn't strike me as a remedial math class.'

Dillon turned to look at her. She thought he looked just a little annoyed. She wondered if it was her comment or the fact that she'd overheard his arrangements that had displeased him.

Geneva nodded. 'Heidi's old one is upstairs.'

'We'll be touring the plant this morning, but if the room could be available by afternoon I'd appreciate it. We'll move the blackboard downstairs, of course—don't worry about that.'

'I'll make sure everything's ready.' Geneva smiled at Heidi and went on into the dining-room.

Heidi waited till her mother was out of earshot. 'Dillon, I'd like to talk to you.'

'That makes for a change.' He sounded perfectly calm. 'You've been pretty quiet for a couple of days now.'

'About the Works——'

'Are you still fixed on that subject? I told you, I don't know what I'm going to do.'

'I remember what you said. Before you take the advice you're being given to close the Works——'

His eyebrows arched. 'I beg your pardon?'

'Oh, don't play dumb,' Heidi said sharply. 'It's pretty obvious these people aren't your Thursday night poker club. Besides, I was in the solarium last night while you were on the terrace.'

He tensed just a little; she could see the muscles in his jaw tighten. But his voice was lazy. 'And you heard Adrienne's advice? She's one of the best accountants in the country, you know.'

'I don't doubt she's good at keeping track of details,' Heidi said tartly. 'But that's beside the point, isn't it? Before you close down the Works, please think about all the people you'd be hurting. We need this plant, Dillon. We need these jobs.'

Was that a spark of sympathy in his eyes? 'It can't go on the way it is, Heidi.'

'Of course it can't. But why don't we look at who's to blame for the shape it's in? You're the reason it was stumbling when you bought it, and you haven't put a penny into it since. You've drained its resources by selling equipment and not replacing it. Your best workers have moved on because they know you're not committed to this plant.'

'You make me wonder how it's managed to limp along till now,' Dillon murmured. 'By the way, just to get things clear, are you offering me some sort of enticement in return for keeping it open?'

Heidi's face flamed. 'That's disgusting!'

His gaze moved slowly over her. 'Now why should you assume I had something off-color and personal in mind? Perhaps I'm thinking of a rebate on my property tax.' His voice was smooth.

Heidi gritted her teeth and glared at him. 'Would you at least consider selling it instead?'

His tone didn't change, but she thought she saw an interested gleam in his eyes. 'That depends. Who's interested in buying? You?'

'I know someone who might be. I don't think I should tell you who till I check with——'

'In that case, I'm not interested in selling.'

Heidi bit her lip. 'Masters,' she said finally. 'The chicken tycoon.'

Dillon folded his arms across his chest. 'Now I've heard everything,' he drawled.

'It's not as crazy as it sounds. If he builds the chicken plant, he'll need a lot of boxes and shipping cartons. And he told me himself that it looked as if you were in trouble, and...' Her voice trailed off.

'And he could pick the Works up at a bargain-basement price?'

'Something like that,' Heidi admitted.

'That's quite a breathtaking offer.' His voice was dry. 'On the whole, I don't think I'm interested in pursuing it.'

'You'd rather close it? Won't you even consider the alternative?'

'Are you so sure Masters would be a sympathetic employer?'

Heidi bit her lip. 'Any jobs are better than none at all,' she said stubbornly.

'Perhaps you're right.' Dillon looked over Heidi's shoulder. 'I'll think it over.'

She turned to see what he was watching; Adrienne was coming out of the dining-room, swinging her portfolio.

Dillon said abruptly, 'We'll talk about this later.'

'Certainly.' Heidi turned away.

'Oh, and Heidi—If I hear rumors, I'll know where they started.'

She stopped and faced him. 'If there are rumors, Dillon, it won't be my fault. People have been speculating about your intentions for a year, and I'm simply not interested enough in what you do to comment about it.'

'Oh, aren't you? Then why even ask whether I intend to close the plant?'

'The Works, yes—I'm interested in that. But not in you.'

As she swung around toward the door again, Heidi saw Adrienne's face slacken with astonishment.

In full daylight, Heidi thought, the woman looked a great deal older than she had last night in the flattering glow of candles. A good deal older—and a whole lot less certain of herself.

That was a tiny bit of comfort.

CHAPTER SEVEN

HEIDI was more than halfway through the list of prospects Mitch had asked her to approach, but that morning her progress was slow, and she had to double-check everything she did. She kept thinking about Dillon, and how he had so coolly declined even to think about selling the Works. She had to admit that Masters' offer, if it came through, wasn't likely to be a glamorous one, but what else could Dillon expect?

When Mitch—finally back from his business trip—came into her office at mid-morning and picked up the packet she was working on, it was all Heidi could do not to snap at him. The last thing she needed was her boss looking over her shoulder and second-guessing every choice she made!

'Why are you sending a leaflet about our elementary schools to the president of a chain of retirement homes?' he asked mildly.

'Because his corporation has a foster-grandparent program in most of its facilities. They adopt school classes and help them with their lessons.'

'Oh. Good job, Heidi.'

'Besides, maybe he has kids of his own.'

'You mean you don't know how old they are and what they like to play with?' Mitch teased. He put the packet down and perched on the corner of her desk. 'You know, I still can't believe what you told me about Masters wanting the moon from the city.'

'Believe it,' Heidi said shortly. She sealed the package and picked up the next letter.

'Well, I talked to the mayor this morning, and we concluded that maybe we could do a little better than the standard concessions. Not as good as he seems to want, but maybe——'

'Mitch!'

'It would be a rotten shame to lose that plant, Heidi. The payroll would be in the millions every year.'

'I know. But if you submit to blackmail from one corporation...'

She paused. Just this morning, when Dillon had said he wasn't especially interested in Masters' offer, Heidi had blithely said that any jobs were better than none. And it was true; Masters' employees would buy houses and cars and haircuts and craft supplies—and all of Fairview's businesses would benefit. Perhaps Mitch wasn't being unrealistic after all.

'He'd eventually hire more than three hundred workers,' Mitch said. 'And you know if the Works closes we'll need every job we can scrape up.'

So much for the idea of me starting rumors, Heidi thought. Dillon would probably blame her for it, though. She probably ought to try to squelch the story; even though at the moment the closing certainly looked likely, it wasn't yet fact. 'There's always talk, Mitch.'

'Maybe that's all it is,' he said gloomily. 'But you know Ken Ferris turned down a seat on the planning council a couple of weeks ago.'

'Yes. I thought he said he was terribly busy at the Works...' Her voice trailed off as she realized what Mitch was getting at.

'He did say that, but he doesn't look all that busy, does he? I got to thinking that maybe he doesn't plan to be here long, and he didn't want to go to all the trouble of taking on an unpopular job and then resign in a few months.'

Or maybe, Heidi thought, he knows that he'll soon be very busy indeed, terminating employees and cleaning out the last of the equipment. It was hard to believe Ken Ferris wouldn't know about the recommendations made for his plant—he must have been involved in making them.

Mitch forced a smile. 'But that's pessimistic, and we don't allow ourselves to think negatively in this office, right? By the way, why didn't you tell me Dillon Archer is in town?'

Heidi slid a stack of materials into a manila envelope. 'Didn't I?'

'No, you didn't. I made a fool of myself at City Hall when I didn't recognize him.'

'He was at City Hall? This morning?'

'Big as life, waiting to talk to the mayor.' He slid off the desk. 'When you're finished with these, Heidi, I've got another list and some follow-up calls to make.'

'Sure, Mitch.' But she was hardly listening, and she sat idle for several minutes, staring at the pamphlets on her desk without seeing them. What did Dillon want from the mayor? Not special favors for the Works, she thought, for if the plant was closing it wouldn't make any difference. Or did he think he could make the deal more enticing for a potential buyer, and get a higher price, if he could throw in some extras courtesy of the city? He hadn't said he wouldn't consider a sale at all, just that Masters' interest didn't appeal to him. And even that might change if the offer was better than he expected. He'd said he would think about it...

Heidi shook her head in confusion. The whole thing was getting too complicated for her. The implications would take more time and energy to figure out than playing three-dimensional chess against a computer—and she'd never been any good at that, either.

She had lunch with Callie Martin at a little coffee shop just down the street from the craft store. Callie settled into the booth with a sigh. 'You don't know how nice it is to get off my feet. Not that I'm complaining about business, you understand. I just mean it's nice to get out of there for a little while.'

'How's the new clerk working out?'

Callie shrugged. 'I wouldn't want to leave the store in her hands for any length of time just yet, but it's a relief to get out for lunch at least.'

Both of them ordered tenderloin sandwiches, and Heidi was stirring sweetener into her iced tea when Callie added, 'Though perhaps I shouldn't have hired anyone just yet. If things keep up the way they're going at the Works, Dad may be out of a job and I'll probably end up hiring my mother to work in the store so they can put food on the table.' She looked at her coffee glumly.

Heidi was glad she didn't have to meet Callie's eyes just then. She couldn't lie to her friend—but what was the truth?

'Sorry,' Callie said. 'I didn't mean to beg for sympathy. If anybody's had it rough over the Works, it's you. Watch out—there's trouble behind you. Here comes Barry.'

Barry Evans pulled up a chair and sat down. 'Heidi, I need to talk to you.' He didn't even nod at Callie.

'Won't you join us?' Callie said sweetly. She looked, Heidi thought, as if she'd like to dump her coffee in Barry's lap.

'Not for lunch,' Barry said. 'I just came in to get a take-out order, and it'll be ready in a minute. Heidi, my fiancée wants to have our engagement party at Lilac Hill.'

Callie's eyebrows soared.

Heidi tried to ignore her. 'I'm sure we can handle that. When, and how many people?'

Barry waved a careless hand. 'Lord, I don't know. That's all up to her and her mother—I just wanted to warn you they'd be calling.'

Callie rolled her eyes.

Heidi said, 'We'll come up with something nice, Barry. If you're worried about the budget . . .'

'Not on that affair. That's her father's problem. But she wants to have the rehearsal dinner there too.'

And since the rehearsal dinner was the responsibility of the groom's family, Heidi concluded, the bill for that party would be Barry's.

Callie leaned across the table with a confiding air. 'How about a wienie roast? It's the newest thing—upscale brides are doing it in all the cities. I heard about one in Central Park just last month—even the muggers wore black tie, and they served deli potato salad and baked beans and pickle spears with the wienies...'

Heidi had to bite her lip to keep from smiling. 'I'll talk to Kate, Barry. She does some very elegant main dishes which really aren't expensive at all. I'm sure we can come up with something that will satisfy you.'

Barry grinned. 'Thanks, Heidi. You're a gem.' He dropped his voice. 'You know, I often think of the way things should have been.'

Callie choked, and managed to turn the sound into a sort of awkward cough. She didn't recover till after Barry had picked up his lunch order and disappeared down the street. '"The way things should have been,"' she said with disgust. 'That egocentric idiot! Why don't you just squash him like the insect he is, Heidi?'

'What good would it do? It would make me look cruel. And he was hurt by the whole thing too, you know. He went from a comfortable job with a great future to——'

'Don't forget his expectations of marrying the boss's daughter,' Callie said rudely. 'What a shame he's such a cheapskate—that could be quite a party if he weren't.' She waited till the waitress had set their food down and added softly, 'Remember the picnics your mother used to have every year for all the employees at the Works and their families?'

Heidi smiled. 'The garden parties? Mother would never refer to them as mere picnics. That was a tradition my grandfather started, you know.' Thoughtfully she spread mustard across her sandwich. 'I used to hate those parties when I was a kid. I couldn't understand why Mother didn't make everyone stay in the tents she put up on the lawn. Instead they wandered over the whole estate. They trampled over my favorite spots, and the kids made so much noise they scared all the wildlife away for days. And she always made me lead the games.'

'Tough life you had, sweetie.' Callie's voice dripped mock-sympathy.

Heidi smiled. 'Well, it seemed like it at the time.' She hadn't even thought about the annual garden parties for a long time. There hadn't been a party for a couple of years. Last summer, with George Cameron gone and the Works so changed, nobody had even considered it.

But those gatherings were precious memories. Everyone had seemed to have fun; seldom did any employee miss the annual blowout at Lilac Hill. They had always put rowboats on the lake and had a fishing contest for the kids. The tennis court and swimming-pool had been in use all day. And Heidi would never forget her father pitching horseshoes with some of his line workers, and swapping a few off-color jokes when he was certain Geneva wasn't within earshot...

She frowned a little.

'Is something wrong with your sandwich?' Callie asked.

Heidi shook her head. But she hardly tasted her tenderloin, for she was too busy exploring the germ of an idea.

It was crazy. It was unethical. In fact, it was downright unscrupulous. But it just might be worth a try.

Heidi was on the telephone not long after lunch when the secretary put her head in and said, 'Gentleman to see you, Heidi.'

She caught a glimpse, over Betty's shoulder, of a tall, lean man with dark hair, and wanted to groan. She had almost forgotten Dillon saying this morning that they'd talk later about Masters' interest in the Works. She had expected it to be a whole lot later—and maybe never. Shouldn't he still be occupied with his advisory board this afternoon? If they'd toured the Works this morning, as he'd said they were going to, they ought to have a lot to talk about.

Of course, if everyone felt the same way Adrienne Collins did, it might have been a very short tour and a very brief conference. Maybe Dillon had already been persuaded.

She cupped her hand over the telephone mouthpiece. 'Tell him I'll be with him in a moment, Betty,' she said, and frowned. Right now, this very instant, it wasn't too late to back out. But if she proceeded ... She took a deep breath and uncovered the phone. 'All right, that's barbecued beef and fried chicken for four hundred, and all the trimmings, delivered to Lilac Hill by six o'clock Wednesday evening. Oh, and make sure there's a lot of iced tea and soft drinks, because it's supposed to be warm that day.'

'I've got it,' said the lady on the other end of the line. 'I'm happy to help you however I can, Heidi.'

As she put down the phone, Heidi felt an odd little thrill in her bones—a combination of exhilaration and panic, now that it was too late to back out.

She went to the door of her office. Dillon had taken a chair and was waiting patiently, apparently absorbed in watching the traffic on Main Street. He didn't even look up.

'I'm free now,' Heidi said finally.

'That's a leading remark, you know. It gives me all kinds of hope.' He didn't seem to expect a reply. That was just as well; Heidi wasn't about to encourage him.

Dillon looked around her office with obvious interest. Heidi took the chair behind her desk and watched him.

'I'm surprised,' he said finally, and sat down across from her. 'There's not as much of your personality displayed as I'd have thought. It's not at all like your bedroom at Lilac Hill.'

'You mean the bedroom I used to occupy? If you came all the way downtown to tell me that, Dillon——'

'In fact, this office is just short of bare. Does that mean Lilac Hill reflects your mother's taste, not yours?'

'No, it means the Ambassadors don't believe in spending precious money to redecorate on a whim. This room was painted—oh, probably ten years ago. They'll do it again just as soon as it needs it.'

He smiled at that. 'You could bring in your own things, though.'

'This is supposed to be only a part-time job, and probably a temporary one. If it starts to look permanent, I'll think about surrounding myself with my treasures. Now if there's something I can do for you, Dillon...'

He reached into the breast pocket of his jacket and took out his wallet. 'I hope you'll take my check today,' he said. 'I seem to be running into a shortage of cash.'

'I'm not surprised,' Heidi said drily. 'Look, Dillon, I told you days ago that ordinary business arrangements are fine. You can pay the bill at the end of your stay.'

'That's very sweet, but I wouldn't expect you to take the chance of me coming up short at the end.' He propped the check-book on his knee and began to write without hurry.

'Oh, I'm not taking chances.' Heidi's voice was sweet. 'I checked your credit rating last week.'

He paused as if she'd startled him, and smiled. Then he tore the check out and passed it across the desk.

The sheer size of it made her blink. 'Just exactly what is this for?'

'Five rooms for three nights.'

Through Wednesday night, she calculated. Originally he'd told Geneva his 'friends' would be at Lilac Hill for a full week; things must be moving along faster than he had expected. 'Dillon...'

'That's at my special rate, of course.' Irony rang in his words. 'Plus the meals.'

Heidi bit her lip.

Dillon capped his pen and put it back in his pocket. 'I'll let you know after that how much longer we'll be staying.'

She gave up and put the check in her desk drawer. 'I'm glad you've at least given up the fiction that you're all just great friends.'

'Oh, some of us are,' he said easily.

Like him and Adrienne Collins, Heidi thought. That ought to put her in her place. 'And that's why you're paying all the bills, I'm sure.'

'Of course.'

Heidi shuffled some papers. 'I happened to talk to Masters a while ago.'

'Oh? Called him up, did you?'

His tone was casual, but Heidi knew better, for she'd seen the flare of interest in his eyes. 'As a matter of fact, he called me. I told him I'd mentioned his interest in the Works to you.'

'He didn't happen to give you a price, did he?'

'Of course not. I have no intention of getting involved in negotiations. That's none of my business.'

'Funny you should say that,' Dillon mused.

Heidi lost her temper. 'I'm just trying to help everybody. If there isn't anything else, Dillon, I've got a lot of work to do today.'

'That will take care of it.' He rose. 'No, wait—there is one more thing. Where can I get a photocopier and a fax machine?'

'The office supply place is right down the block.' She pointed. 'Don't you have all you need at the plant?'

'I want them delivered to Lilac Hill.'

'That ought to raise some eyebrows.'

'I don't see why. I'll just tell the salesman they're a gift for you.'

Heidi rolled her eyes. 'I'm sure he'll get a thrill out of that. Wouldn't it be easier to have your conference at the plant? It would be a lot more comfortable than the music-room at Lilac Hill—Mother's not kidding about the furniture—and the equipment's already set up.'

He just looked at her for a long moment, and then said politely, 'As a general principle, Heidi, I believe there is no such thing as a dumb question. But you're forcing me to reconsider the matter.'

She colored a little. Perhaps it *had* been a stupid thing to ask. 'All right, so you don't want any of your employees eavesdropping on the debate. I can understand that. But don't think you're eliminating talk—everybody in town is already wondering why you're here, and you can't keep your cohorts hidden for long, either. Mitch wasn't back in Fairview two hours before he heard that the Works is closing.'

'Mitch? That's your boss?'

'You met him at City Hall this morning,' she reminded him, and watched him carefully. Would Dillon look just a bit uncomfortable at having to admit he'd been talking to the mayor?

But he didn't even blink. 'So he's been hearing stories. I wonder who he's been talking to?'

'Well, don't look at me as if I'm responsible for the rumors,' Heidi said tartly, 'because I'm not.'

Dillon smiled. 'I'd hate to think you were, because there are some dandies going around about us.' He opened the door of her office. 'See you at dinner.'

Heidi was out of her chair and around the desk before she stopped to think, but Dillon moved so quickly that

he was on the sidewalk outside the Ambassadors'
building before she caught up with him. 'What do you
mean?'

'Dinner? Oh, you mean the rumors. Just the run-of-
the-mill speculation about whether we're sleeping
together. I didn't bother to get the details, because I don't
generally pass along gossip. But if you'd like to make it
true...'

'Then I suppose you'd enjoy telling the whole world!'

His gaze flicked over her. He seemed particularly to
appreciate the tendrils of hair which had come loose from
her French twist and were stirring in the summer breeze.
She half expected that he'd reach out to smooth the loose
strands back into place, but he didn't.

'Of course not,' he said, sounding a little surprised at
the question. 'Then I'd really keep the details to myself.'

'Well, that's some comfort. Not that I'm interested.'

Dillon smiled a little. 'Yes, you are, the same way I
am—even though my better judgement tells me you're
really not a safe woman to be interested in.'

'Then perhaps you'd better keep your distance,' Heidi
snapped.

'But that wouldn't be any fun at all, would it?'

Before she could read his intentions, he'd bent his head
and brushed a kiss across her lips. The contact was light
and fleeting, but the sensation burned all the way to
Heidi's bones.

It wasn't excitement she was feeling, however, she told
herself. And it certainly wasn't passion. It was simple
fury at being treated so lightly in the middle of Main
Street, with heaven knew how many people watching.
If he'd *wanted* to cause talk, he couldn't have chosen a
better way to do it. Maybe he didn't pass along gossip,
but he knew how to cause it.

Well, two could play that game. After all, she'd actually considered starting a very similar rumor herself,
just to embarrass him. She'd been right about how much

good it would do, too—so perhaps there were more effective methods.

'You know,' she said thoughtfully, 'after that display, everyone in Fairview will believe I'm in a position to know the truth about what's going to happen at the Works. If I wanted to feed the rumors that it's closing——'

'But you won't.' There was not a shred of doubt in Dillon's voice.

'Why wouldn't I? Maybe I think people deserve fair warning, and since it's likely to happen——'

'Because that would leave me with no choice at all. I'd have to shut the Works down then, or make you look like a liar.' He slid a finger down a loose strand of her hair, tucking it behind her ear. 'And I couldn't make you look bad, Heidi—not with what we've meant to each other.' He smiled down at her and then strolled off toward the office supply store.

Heidi almost stamped her foot on the sidewalk before she recalled where she was and retreated in disarray to her office.

The sheer nerve of the man made her see red. 'What we've meant to each other', indeed! And as for him making it sound that if the Works closed, it would be her fault...

If she didn't end up by throwing Dillon Archer out of a top-floor window, it would be a miracle.

Heidi tried to tackle her bookkeeping on Wednesday afternoon, partly because it genuinely needed doing—the mortgage payment was due on Thursday, and she hadn't written the check yet—and partly because whenever she closeted herself in the top-floor playroom everybody left her alone. Guests never came near the top floor, and Kate and Geneva knew better than to disturb her for anything short of disaster when she was wrestling with Lilac Hill's finances.

But within half an hour Heidi had forgotten to enter two checks in the register, and when she ended up tearing open an envelope to make sure she'd paid the right amount and enclosed the correct paperwork she gave up. She pushed her chair back, staring out the window to where the picnic would begin in an hour or so.

It would not be like the elegant garden parties of her memories, when they had devoted a whole day to entertainment and wonderful food. This year there would be no tents, no contests or organized games, no rowboats on the lake. Of course, she wasn't trying to reproduce those glorious days; they were past, and nothing could bring them back. But if her plan worked out, there would be one thing just like those wonderful parties of old, and that would make the time and the cost worthwhile.

And if it didn't work out… Her stomach tightened in terrified anticipation.

She heard footsteps on the stairs and hastily tugged the check-book open. She was writing a draft to cover the mortgage payment when Dillon appeared. 'I'm very busy,' she said, without looking up.

'I can see that.' He settled on to a bench near by. 'I'll just sit here quietly and enjoy the view and wait for you to finish.'

Heidi shot a glance at him. He was not looking out the window, but at her. He seemed calm enough, but the hair on the back of her neck prickled in warning. Had he heard about the picnic?

Even if he had, she didn't think he'd be suspicious, for he'd have no reason to connect the event with Heidi, or even with Lilac Hill. Ken Ferris's secretary—who had also worked for George Cameron, and therefore remembered Heidi with affection—had promised to post signs in the plant inviting all employees to a picnic at Fairview's largest city park. But Heidi hadn't even taken the secretary completely into her confidence; she herself had stopped at the park on her way home from work today and tacked up posters announcing that the party had been moved to Lilac Hill.

She'd been most worried about Ken Ferris, who might wonder why no one seemed to know who'd organized the company picnic. But as it happened, Ken had spent much of Tuesday and Wednesday at Lilac Hill. And Dillon, so far as she knew, hadn't been close to the plant again. He'd been closeted with his experts in the music-room for hours at a stretch.

Heidi wanted to ask what conclusions they were reaching, but she didn't think she'd get an answer. And she could see for herself that the conference wasn't going easily.

They came out for little except meals, and then they appeared to be worn and exhausted—except for Dillon, who never quite lost the ironic gleam in his eyes. He looked as if he was just stepping out for intermission from some very enjoyable play. Heidi wondered what Adrienne Collins thought of that. Was she ready to eat her words about how much fun it was to work Dillon round to her point of view?

And why was Adrienne having so much trouble, anyway? Heidi frowned. If closing the plant was clearly the best option, why was Dillon delaying his decision? Was he simply holding off to give Masters a chance to get his bid in before it was too late? Or waiting to see what the mayor might do? Extra concessions for the Works would help make up for some of the benefits Masters wanted—but wasn't likely to get—for his chicken plant...

Dillon moved across the room to stand behind her chair, looking over her shoulder. 'What's wrong?'

'Oh, I've got the check-book messed up.' She closed it with a snap. 'I'll straighten it out later. What brought you up here, anyway?'

'I came to let you know that Adrienne left this afternoon, and the Hales will be going tomorrow. Their work's done.'

Heidi swallowed hard. 'It's decided, then.' And it wasn't too hard to guess what the decision was. If Dillon's accountant was leaving, it didn't appear there was a sale in the works. If there was, he'd want her around to help negotiate the price, wouldn't he?

Heidi told herself it shouldn't be a shock; she had known how slim a chance of survival the Works had. But she hadn't realized till now that she had been clinging so fiercely to the last speck of hope.

'Yes.' Nothing more—but then perhaps he felt there was nothing more to say. Dillon's hands came to rest on her shoulders, gently massaging.

The reassuring touch was more than Heidi could bear. He seemed to be trying to tell her that he understood, that it would be all right. But if he truly understood, Heidi thought furiously, he'd do things differently. And it was easy for him to say everything would be all right— after all, he'd be leaving the problems behind.

She shrugged his hands off her shoulders and stood up. 'What about the others? Tweedledum and Tweedledee—and you?'

She didn't realize she'd let the nicknames slip out till Dillon's eyebrows rose. 'The three of us will be staying another few days.'

'Just long enough to tie up loose ends,' Heidi said.

'That's about it. I do have a dozen other plants to run, and several of them could do with attention at the moment.'

From the top of the stairs, Geneva called, 'Heidi? I just came back from my bridge club, and Kate says you gave her the afternoon off and told her you'd take care of dinner. Do you want to tell me what's going on and why you're up here instead of doing something about it?'

Heidi closed her eyes in a futile attempt to ward off the pain in her temples. In the shock of hearing Dillon's announcement, she'd forgotten that within minutes a catering truck would drive up and several hundred people would begin to assemble for a picnic. A company picnic—for a company which was going out of business, and a whole lot of employees who in a few weeks would have no jobs to celebrate.

What a party it's going to be, she thought grimly.

CHAPTER EIGHT

THE picnic had seemed like such a good idea, even if
the notion had been born of desperation. Even though
Dillon was a hard-headed businessman who kept both
eyes on the bottom line, he wasn't completely insensitive. Surely if he was forced to face his employees
outside the factory, to meet their families, to see them
all as people and not mere office supplies, he could not
simply turn his back on them. At least, that was the way
Heidi had reasoned the situation through.

But she'd been wrong. She'd let her own hypnotic attraction for the man blind her. What a dreamer she'd
been to let herself forget for even an instant how he'd
treated her father—ruthlessly undercutting prices,
shamelessly stealing customers, then twisting what little
remained of the business out of George Cameron's
hands. Why should he feel any more compassion for the
workers than he had for the owner of the business?

And now that the decision had been made, it was too
late anyway. Even if Heidi's brainstorm was successful
in striking some deep-down undercurrent of compassion
in Dillon's heart, it wasn't going to do any good. The
whole party was an expensive exercise in futility.

No, she thought with determination. Even if it didn't
make a difference in the outcome where the Works was
concerned, the party was not a waste. He'd at least have
to face his employees and recognize the damage he was
doing by closing the Works. Even if not a single job was
saved, there would be just a little satisfaction in making
him admit the harshness of what he was doing.

Geneva said, sharply, 'Heidi? Surely you haven't forgotten that you have a half-dozen guests to look after—have you?'

And a few hundred more, too, Heidi almost said. 'Of course not, Mother. I told Kate I'd take care of dinner, and I will. We're having a picnic.'

Geneva looked at her as if Heidi had suddenly broken out in polka dots. Heidi didn't blame her.

'I invited...' Heidi took a deep breath to break the news, and then her resolution faltered under her mother's steady gaze. 'I invited a few extras, you see.'

Geneva's voice was mild. 'Really? And what are you planning to feed them?'

'Barbecued beef and fried chicken. The caterer's truck should be here any minute.'

Dillon said, 'That sounds appetizing. Did you think this up because you had such fun on our last picnic, Heidi?'

The words were innocent enough, but the reminder—in front of her mother—of the kiss they had shared beside the little creek at the furthest corner of Lilac Hill's grounds made Heidi see red. She put her chin up and glared at him. 'Don't you want to know who I've invited to meet you, Dillon? The employees of the Works, that's who. Your employees. All of them.'

Geneva groped for the nearest chair and lowered herself into it. 'Heidi, why?' Her voice was just short of a shriek.

Dillon sat down on the edge of Heidi's desk and folded his arms across his chest.

'Never mind,' Geneva muttered. 'We can go into the reasons later—if I make it through the evening.'

Remorse swept over Heidi. 'Mother, this is my affair. I dreamed it up, and I'll take the responsibility. There's no reason you should have to put yourself out for something that was entirely my idea. I'll tell everyone you had other obligations.'

Geneva shook her head, more in confusion than dis-agreement. 'I should think you'll need all the help you can get.' She stood up again. 'How many are we ex-pecting, Heidi?'

'I figured four hundred. The invitations went out on short notice.'

'You can say that again,' Geneva said under her breath. The sound of her quick footsteps retreating down the stairs was the only sound in the playroom for almost a minute.

The tension in the air was as thick and sticky as mol-asses. Heidi glanced out the window so she wouldn't have to look at Dillon, who was still sitting absolutely mo-tionless on the edge of her desk.

A few cars were coming down the drive, the first of what she was certain would be a lengthy procession. 'I have to get downstairs,' she began.

'What kind of game are you playing?' Dillon's voice was soft and level, but she could feel the underlying hardness like a knife-blade against her throat.

Heidi raised her chin. 'It's not a game, this is dead serious. You've been in Fairview a week now, and as far as I can tell you haven't shown the least bit of interest in anything but machinery and balance sheets. But the Works is more than that, Dillon. It's people, too. The question is whether you have the guts to face those people—and take a good honest look at the pain you'll be causing if you close the plant.'

His eyes narrowed a little. 'That's not what's really bothering you, is it, Heidi?'

She looked up at him for a moment. She wasn't sur-prised to see the cool calculation in his gaze, though ac-tually seeing his expression made her throat ache. She had hoped for a little more warmth, perhaps even some understanding of her motives. 'It's certainly enough,' she said defensively. 'I care about those people. They're like family to me, as they were to my father. And I care about this town——'

He stood up and slowly crossed the room to her. 'Yes. I know all that. So if I was to say that I'll keep the Works open—for a price—what would you tell me?' His voice was low and silky.

Heidi swallowed convulsively. 'I'd say you're being ridiculous.'

'Aren't you even going to ask what kind of price I have in mind?'

Heidi was annoyed with herself; she'd fallen into that suggestive trap before and ended up embarrassing herself and amusing him. 'If you're talking about property tax again, go back and talk to the mayor,' she suggested crisply.

'Oh, no. That's not what I mean this time.' Dillon's hands cupped her face and turned it up to his. 'This is more what I had in mind.'

Her squeak of protest was smothered by the pressure of his lips against hers. It was a fierce and demanding kiss, driven not by violence but by something even more elemental—a desire which spoke to an equally strong longing deep inside her and threatened to rob her of her soul. By the time he was finished, her body didn't seem to work right any more; her hands clutched at the front of his shirt in an effort to hold herself upright and a couple of inches away from him. If it hadn't been for that feeble support, Heidi thought she might have simply melted straight into his body and been lost forever.

'You're addictive,' he whispered as he raised his head. 'Every time I taste you I want more.'

Heidi's voice was little more than a croak. 'Then maybe you should try quitting cold turkey.'

'Or maybe I shouldn't stop until I'm satisfied, no matter what it takes.' He held her a little way from him. 'What about it, Heidi? What if that's my price?'

'You wouldn't do that.' Her voice shook a little.

'You don't think I could be so hard-hearted as to force you into making love with me?' He let her go. 'But you see, I don't believe I'm asking anything so awful. If you'd once stop acting outraged by the idea, you'd realize you're as interested in making love as I am. It's not a matter of force.'

The husky, seductive edge to his voice sent shivers up her spine, and it took tremendous effort for Heidi to stand still. Even though she was no longer in his arms, the magnetic pull he exerted had not diminished, and it was all she could do to keep from creeping closer to him.

She took a deep breath. 'That's not what I meant at all. I think you'd never risk the bottom line just because you wanted a roll in the hay. Now are you coming down to the party? Or shall I tell your employees you're not interested in them?'

Dillon smiled. Heidi was startled; she'd have sworn he was genuinely amused, and she couldn't understand why.

'Oh, I'm coming down.' He brushed a casual hand down the wrinkled front of his shirt, where her fingers had clutched the soft fabric. 'I'll have to change, of course, or people might wonder why I'm so rumpled. But I wouldn't miss this party for the world. Just don't think I'm finished with you, Heidi—we'll take this up again later.'

Heidi stayed as far away from Dillon as she could, but even in a crowd of hundreds she couldn't help being aware of his presence. At any given time, she could have told within a matter of feet where he was on the lawn; the closer he was, the more strongly each nerve-ending tingled. But even when he was at the furthest corner of the lawn, that electrical thrill didn't dissipate. It merely settled into a softer, more even buzz, like a constant ringing in the ears that could be lived with but never ignored.

And just as persistent was the little voice in the back of her mind, repeating that she couldn't possibly be wrong. Dillon had to be bluffing; he couldn't seriously make such an idiotic proposition. Even Masters had said—with somewhat grudging respect—that no matter what the deal Dillon always found a way to make a profit from it.

Unless, this time, he wasn't thinking of profits in terms of mere cash, but more personal benefits...

Heidi shivered a little at the idea, and when a guest noticed she passed it off with a quick remark about the weather not being as warm as had been predicted and hurried off to check on the food supply. She'd seriously underestimated the number of Works employees who would come and bring their families, and she was beginning to wonder if they'd have enough food. How had Geneva ever managed her garden parties—far more complicated than this simple picnic—and enjoyed herself thoroughly all the way through?

Callie Martin's mother, who was sitting on the terrace rail with her paper plate, waved Heidi over. 'What a generous thing to do,' she said, 'to open Lilac Hill to all of us once more.'

'There's nothing really generous about it,' Heidi demurred. 'We're in business, after all.'

'Of course, but it's not as if the house is a public facility or something. This brings back so many memories of your mother's garden parties—pleasant ones for us, but I'm sure it must be painful for you and Geneva to have everyone here.'

'Well, thanks for the kind words, but I don't think this stands any comparison with Mother's parties.' Heidi shifted her weight uneasily. She'd been trying to ignore the vibrations which warned her of Dillon's presence, but there was no way to deny that he was somewhere close at hand. She only hoped he wasn't near enough to be listening.

'Of course this party isn't meant to compete with those extravaganzas. Things are different now, and everyone understands that this was put together on short notice. But still, it's nice to know Mr Archer would go to the trouble to arrange a get-together like this.'

Heidi made a noncommittal noise and glanced around the terrace, trying to think of some excuse to break away without hurting Mrs Martin's feelings. Barely six feet away, Dillon was standing with one foot up on a bench and his elbow propped on his knee. To all appearances, he was listening to one of the Works' employees, but he was watching Heidi, and the gleam in his eyes was ironic. He'd heard all right, and he was enjoying the appreciation of not only Mrs Martin but all the people who supposed they were his guests.

It was almost funny, Heidi thought, that the only person willing to give her full credit for the party was the one who planned to hold her completely responsible when it was all over. 'Don't think I'm finished with you,' he'd said. 'We'll take this up again later.'

Mrs Martin leaned closer. 'I feel much better about the future of the plant now,' she confided, 'with the interest he's showing in all of us, and the length of time he's spent here. I don't mind telling you we've been worried, with all the talk about the Works closing.'

Heidi could feel her stomach sinking to her toes. She'd had such good intentions in arranging this picnic—but what if the only thing she accomplished with her grand-stand gesture was to give a false sense of hope to the Works' employees? A lot of help that would be, in the long run, when the announcement was finally made!

Unless Dillon had meant that incredible proposition he'd made. If he was willing to keep the plant open...
'What if that's my price?' he'd said. And if he had been serious, what would her answer be?

He wasn't serious, Heidi told herself. It didn't fit his character. She'd be wise to ignore the whole thing. But despite her best intentions, her gaze slid back to his face.

Mrs Martin saw him too. 'It's nice that he even bothered to find out about the traditional summer parties,' she said. 'I wonder if he intends to have another next year? If he does, I'd be happy to help, Heidi. I know how much work these affairs can be.'

Next year, Heidi thought bleakly. But there wasn't going to be a next year—for the plant or the employees or the picnic. Unless...

Dillon was moving closer. She could feel the increased electricity in the hair at the nape of her neck. 'That will be up to Mr Archer, of course,' Heidi said quietly.

Dillon's hand came to rest, lightly but possessively, on her shoulder. 'No,' he said gently. 'Remember? It's up to you.' He smiled at Mrs Martin. 'I've put Miss Cameron in charge of all that.'

Mrs Martin raised one eyebrow as she looked from one of them to the other. 'I see,' she said mildly. 'Perhaps it's even more like old times than I'd thought.'

Heidi tried to ignore the hot flush of embarrassed color in her cheeks. She knew what Mrs Martin was thinking; the woman was imagining wedding-bells. But Heidi could think only of the kind of deal Dillon had offered. There was nothing less like the devoted love her parents had shared, and the idea of comparing the two things made her feel almost ill.

'If you'll excuse us, I'm going to make sure Heidi eats something,' Dillon confided to Mrs Martin. He drew Heidi toward the caterer's truck. 'Besides, I want another piece of chicken myself.'

'Have my share,' Heidi muttered. 'I think I'd choke on it.'

'Aren't you enjoying yourself, my dear?' His tone was solicitous. 'Would you like to talk about whatever it is you have on your mind?'

Heidi shook her head. 'You seem to be having a good time.'

'Oh, didn't you want me to? Sorry to disappoint you, but I figured since I was no doubt going to get the bill for this I might as well appreciate the party.'

'You won't get the bill. I paid for it all out of the profits from your stay.'

'You overcharged me that much, hmm? And blew it all on food for the masses?' He shook his head sadly. 'That's no way to run a business, Heidi. You can't ignore the bottom line because of a quirky idea.'

Heidi stared up at him. 'You have a weird sense of humor, Archer, you know that? This whole song and dance of trying to get me into bed with you is just so much hot air. You're bluffing, and you can cut it out right now.'

Dillon paused with a chicken leg halfway to his mouth. 'I've been known to bluff, on occasion,' he admitted. 'But what makes you so certain this is one of those times?'

'Because you really mean what you said just now—about bottom lines and quirky ideas. You're far too hard-headed to put a fleeting physical pleasure before the best interests of your business.'

Dillon smiled. 'I'll have to dissect that one before I decide whether it was a compliment or not.' He bit into his chicken.

'Let me reassure you. It wasn't.'

'Yet it has elements which are decidedly flattering. You do realize how endlessly fascinating you are, don't you, Heidi?' He discarded the chicken bone and wiped his fingers. 'You make it extremely difficult to ignore you and pay attention to my guests. But of course I must—you'd be very disappointed in me if I didn't, wouldn't you?'

He strolled off. But this time the electricity tingling through her nerves didn't dissipate with distance.

*　　*　　*

As dusk fell, the guests who had wandered off toward the lake or the far corners of the estate reappeared. Almost automatically, it seemed, they gathered near the terrace, where Dillon was sitting on a table, drinking coffee and holding court.

Heidi decided not to watch, so she headed for the caterer's truck to discuss her bill. It wasn't going to be a happy consultation, she figured, since they'd far exceeded the crowd she'd expected and had to send back for extra supplies. And how she was going to explain the cost to Geneva... Maybe she could negotiate a payment plan, and take care of it herself from her Ambassadors' paycheck, and her mother would never have to know the extent of her folly.

She'd been a sheer idiot in the first place to think that she could seriously affect the course of Dillon's decisions.

Or was it possible that she could?

'What if that's my price?' Once again his words echoed in her mind, and once again she told herself to stop being a fool. He hadn't actually made any sort of offer, or demand. The only thing he'd done was ask a question. He hadn't meant it seriously. If she were to walk up to him right now and say she'd pay the price he asked, there was a good chance Dillon would throw back his head and laugh, delighted that she'd been so amusing as to take him seriously.

Though on the other hand...

The memory of that kiss this afternoon up in the playroom flooded over her, a memory as scorching as the kiss itself had been. There had been nothing playful about that caress, nothing teasing. He had kissed her as hungrily as if indeed he felt the craving he'd claimed. And if that was the truth...

Not that she was going to find out which way he'd react, for there were no circumstances whatever in which she would agree to make the deal he had so carelessly proposed.

The still harried crew was trying to clean up, and the caterer made it plain—as pleasantly as possible—that Heidi was getting in the way. 'I haven't any idea what the final bill will be, anyway,' she said. 'I made three extra trips back to the restaurant, and till I've taken inventory of what we used...'

Heidi nodded. 'Let me know.' She stepped out of the truck just as Dillon began to speak.

His voice was almost commanding, obviously pitched to carry across the lawn to the furthest corner. Heidi was more than a hundred feet away, but the deep, rich tone stopped her in her tracks. 'Since so many of you are together,' he said, 'I'd like to address the rumors that have been going around. There's been a lot of talk about the Works closing, and I'd like you to get your information straight from me.'

The last remaining buzz of conversation died into utter stillness. In the darkness, the cicadas hummed, and under a tree a cricket rasped. But there was no human noise, and in the lighted circle around the terrace no one moved.

'I'm sure it's no surprise to any of you that the Works is not a healthy business and it hasn't been for some time,' Dillon said.

Heidi thought, He's going to tell them right now. And I'll be lucky not to have a riot in my back yard.

'The reality of the situation is that the plant's production lines are outdated, and the entire operation—buildings and all—is obsolete.'

'And that's the good news,' somebody at the back of the crowd muttered. There was a ripple of bitter laughter.

'To add to the problem,' Dillon went on, 'demand for the products we make is going down as our customers are switching to other kinds of packaging.'

Gloom settled across the watching faces in a cloud so heavy it was almost visible.

Dillon's voice softened, but the silence was so complete that no one had trouble hearing. 'Closing the plant is a sensible choice.'

There was a wordless whimper from the crowd, the painful moan of a mortally wounded animal. Heidi could feel the same ache in her own throat. She closed her eyes and bit her lip hard.

Dillon straightened his shoulders. 'At least that's what my board of directors decided,' he said almost cheerfully.

Heidi half expected someone to pick up a rock and toss it at him. She'd have liked to do it herself.

'But after a great deal more thought and discussion, it isn't what we're going to do after all. The Works won't close.'

There was a gasp, and then a sound that was half-sob, half-cheer, and the crowd surged toward Dillon.

He raised both hands as if to hold them back, and the somber note crept back into his voice. 'I'm not in a position to tell you any more than that at the moment. I can't promise that employment will increase. I can't even promise that it won't go down a little more. We're looking at options just now. We'll be bringing in some new machinery, probably some new product lines.'

Heidi was dazed. If it weren't for the reaction of the crowd, she'd have thought she was hallucinating. He'd said the decision had been made...

At least I was right about one thing, she thought. He had only been bluffing about her going to bed with him in return for the Works' continued life. If he'd been serious, he'd never have given up his advantage by making this announcement.

She frowned a little. So, now that she knew he'd only been teasing, why didn't she feel incredible relief?

Dillon was still talking. 'It's important that you understand this. The future of the Works depends in large part on you. It isn't going to be easy. Retooling takes time, and retraining takes dedication. If we all pull together, this plant will survive, and probably grow. If we don't, we'll be having this same conversation a few years down the road—with a different ending.'

There were nods of understanding here and there, and determined looks in the crowd. A few people gathered around Dillon to pursue questions; most began to drift thoughtfully off toward their cars. A few stopped to thank Heidi; the majority were too preoccupied to notice her.

The caterers' trucks pulled away, and gradually the party faded. Half an hour later Heidi caught her mother dragging a bag of garbage around the grounds, picking up the last loose cups and napkins, and made Geneva go upstairs to rest.

It was a long time before Heidi herself considered sleep. For one thing, now that the tension was mostly gone, she realized she was starving. After the last guests had said goodbye, she headed for the kitchen.

'All that food, and what I wouldn't give for a bite of barbecued beef right now,' she muttered as she raided Kate's refrigerator for sandwich makings. 'That's the most expensive single meal I'll probably ever see, and I didn't even sample it.'

'I think, in the circumstances, it's my bill,' Dillon said from behind her.

Startled, Heidi banged her head on the refrigerator shelf. 'What are you doing here? After all the chicken you put away——'

'What kind of a bribe would it take to get a fresh pot of coffee? Your caterer has a good touch with food, but her coffee could remove paint.'

Heidi shook her head. 'It wasn't the coffee that was upsetting your stomach, it was the speech you were making.' But she reached for the pot and filled it with water.

'Was that your impression? I thought it went rather well.'

Heidi flipped the switch to start the coffee brewing and turned back to her sandwich, adding sliced turkey and a leaf of lettuce. 'It's a good thing they'd eaten all the food by the time you started to talk, or you'd have had overripe fruit thrown at your head.'

'I thought you'd be happy.'

'At the results, yes—though I'm not quite sure what you really promised. But the technique was cruel.'

'It was calculated,' he countered.

'What's the difference? You could have told them at the outset it was good news, instead of scaring them all to death. I wouldn't have been surprised if someone had had a heart attack on my back lawn tonight.'

Dillon shook his head. 'If I'd just announced new product lines, there'd have been interest and a bit of applause, and everyone would have gone home contented—and kept on much as they've been doing for years.'

'So?'

'That's not good enough, in the circumstances. By leading them up to the cliff and dangling them over the edge——'

'I'd say you did a fine job of that.' She added a layer of cheese to her sandwich and inspected it, then cut it in half and tried a bite.

'And letting them see that it's a very real chasm, I made it plain how important their co-operation is to keep the plant operating.'

'As a motivational technique, that's the lowest, most manipulative——'

'No, it's not. It's the truth. It's going to take a hundred and ten per cent from everybody—from the plant manager to the janitors—to make this work. Better the workers know that up front, so they'll be prepared.'

Heidi thought that one over. 'Maybe. But——'

'It's not a simple call, and the sensible decision would have been to close the whole thing. It would certainly have been the easiest answer.' The coffee-pot sighed, and he reached into the cupboard for a mug. 'Want a cup?'

Heidi shook her head. 'I'm glad you didn't take the easy way,' she said softly.

'I know. If you'd like to show me how grateful you are——'

'I can just stop by your room tonight? No, thanks.'

'It was worth a try,' Dillon mused.

'If you think I'd take you seriously now, after the game you've been playing all evening——'

'You'd better.'

'Oh, stop being ridiculous. You were bluffing before, and you're fishing in the dark now.'

'Not at all. I'm just sure of myself—and of the ultimate results.'

Heidi glared at him. 'You're insufferable!'

'Am I? You're right about a couple of things, you know. I wouldn't base a business decision on a matter of physical pleasure, and I wouldn't blackmail you over the Works, no matter how much fun it is to think about.'

'That's what I said—you were bluffing.'

Dillon grinned. 'Because, you see, I don't have to. Why did you arrange this party, Heidi?'

The abrupt shift of subject startled her. 'I told you this afternoon. I wanted you to face the people you'd be hurting——'

Every line of his face indicated incredulity, but all he said was, 'Think about it, Heidi. I'll see you in the morning...unless, of course, you get lonely tonight.'

'Don't hold your breath,' she said tartly.

Dillon laughed. 'I don't—it's too uncomfortable. I think instead about what our lovemaking will be like. Would you like me to tell you about it?'

'No.'

He said earnestly, 'If you're worried about getting your hopes up too high by fantasizing in advance...'

'I'm not.'

'I agree there's nothing to worry about,' Dillon mused. 'Personally, I think the sky's the limit.'

His words seemed to echo in the kitchen long after he'd gone. Heidi stared at her sandwich and wondered why she even bothered to listen to anything he said. He was an arrogant, insufferable egotist. Just a few nights ago he'd walked Adrienne Collins to her room, and heaven only knew when he'd finally come out. And considering the way he'd been keeping Heidi on edge, implying that the future of the Works depended on her...

If it weren't for the jobs Fairview would lose, she'd have been almost delighted if he'd closed the Works, bulldozed the buildings, and never come back again!

Or would she?

'Why did you arrange this party, Heidi?' The question rang softly in her mind.

The jobs, she thought desperately. Someone had to make him see the pain he was causing.

But it wasn't her business to point that out. And even if she had felt an obligation to interfere, there would have been better, more effective ways—she could have encouraged the Ambassadors to step in, or helped the workers themselves to organize. Instead, she had thrown a party—reminiscent of the old days when the Works and Lilac Hill and the Camerons had been inextricably mixed.

Why?

Not for all the nice reasons she had thought, Heidi admitted. Or at least, not only for those reasons. She had wanted Dillon to see how much the people who worked for him could be hurt by his actions, that was true—but her primary motive hadn't been to protect them. It was to make him want to keep the Works...so she could see him now and then.

Because, if Dillon simply went away, she would hurt forever.

CHAPTER NINE

THE shock of it was enough to make Heidi feel almost physically ill. How had she let such a thing happen? When had she crossed the line from attraction to caring, from liking to...?

She didn't want to use the word loving—it was too much to bear where Dillon was concerned.

When had things changed? When had she let her guard down?

Or perhaps it was more to the point to ask if there had ever been a time when she had been safe from him and the overwhelming sensual power he could exert. Could she, at some point, have simply turned her back and walked away, without suffering everlasting effects?

Probably not, she decided. From the very beginning, from that moment in the solarium when Dillon had held her hand to his heart and looked deep into her eyes, and she had first felt the power of his personality, Heidi had been in danger. Now, looking back, she could see it clearly.

Then, of course, she hadn't even known his name. But finding out who he was hadn't diminished that incredible magnetism. She'd fooled herself into thinking she could spar with him and still keep her emotional balance. And she'd been so certain of herself, of the armor she'd built around her heart, that she had plunged straight into trouble, thinking all the while that her convictions would keep her safe. She'd thought that knowing how Dillon's behavior had affected her father would make her immune to him, no matter what he did.

But she hadn't counted on Dillon and his ability to turn the world upside-down and make it look more sensible that way. She hadn't taken his charm into account. And she certainly hadn't anticipated that the sizzling instantaneous attraction which had sprung so suddenly into existence at their first encounter would continue—and even build—until all he had to do was look at her and she began to question every idea she'd ever held.

Tonight, for instance, even as she'd mingled with her guests, she'd actually been considering the bargain he'd proposed. She'd seriously contemplated the suggestion that she go to bed with him in return for his keeping the Works operating. Or at least that was the excuse she'd given herself. She'd reasoned, at some half-conscious level, that in a sense it would have been a noble sacrifice she was making for the sake of the workers who so needed their jobs.

In fact, it would have been nothing of the sort, if she had acted on that temptation. There would have been no sacrifice involved, and the well-being of the workers would not have been much of a consideration.

It was the underlying motive, the one Heidi had hidden even from herself, which had tantalized her so. If Dillon kept the Works open, he'd have to come to Fairview now and then. And when he came to check on his business...

'Then maybe he'd see me as well,' Heidi murmured.

The confession was painful. She'd always thought of her parents' relationship as an ideal one, and as she'd dated various men she'd compared each new friendship to the Camerons' closeness. Each time she'd found something lacking.

But now she was forced to admit that she would settle for much less than her ideal where Dillon was concerned. She would be contented with scraps of his time. The idea was an uncomfortable one, for she'd never thought of herself as willing to accept less than a man's total devotion. But if bits and pieces were all she could have...

'I'd be better off with nothing,' she said firmly. But she wasn't altogether sure she was convinced.

She knew one thing, however, without any doubt at all. She was lucky Dillon hadn't pressed for an answer to his incredible bargain. At least she had a little time to think it all through, to make a sane decision. And at least it would be her free choice to make, not subject to blackmail—though she was still a little puzzled about why he'd given away such an advantage.

'I wouldn't blackmail you over the Works', he'd said. 'I don't have to'.

That might be true, she admitted. It was uncomfortable to face up to that fact, and even more uncomfortable to realize that he'd seemed to know better than she what she was thinking.

But backing down when he held all the cards seemed an unlikely move for Dillon. After all, he had pressed George Cameron, and his business, to the wall and never let up...

Remember that, Heidi, she reminded herself. Don't let the attraction you feel for Dillon make you forget why we're all in this dilemma in the first place.

Heidi avoided the dining-room the next morning, but she couldn't altogether avoid the guests. When Kate sent her to the basement freezer to get another pound of bacon, Heidi ran headlong into Tweedledum and Tweedledee, who were leaning against the masonry wall of the wine cellar, looking around as if they were lost, and talking about a new way to set up a more efficient production line. She might have been curious at finding them in such an out-of-the-way spot, except for the conversation and the fact that the wine cellar no longer contained anything particularly striking.

'If you're looking for the dining-room,' she pointed out, 'you're one floor too low. Remember?'

They looked a bit embarrassed as they followed her up the stairs once more, emerging into the main foyer just as Mrs Hale came downstairs with a tote bag.

'I'm so glad to get to see you once more before we go,' she told Heidi with a smile. 'How nice it's been to relax at Lilac Hill.'

Heidi wasn't so sure she believed the part about relaxing; Mrs Hale had been involved in all those long meetings in the music-room, too.

'You know,' Heidi said, 'the others' jobs are pretty obvious, now that I know what Dillon's planning. An accountant and a couple of engineers——' She turned to Tweedledum and Tweedledee. 'That is what you guys are, isn't it?'

'Process engineers,' one of them muttered, and they both edged nervously toward the dining-room as if hoping to shut off any further questions.

'Close enough,' Heidi said. 'All that makes perfect sense, with the kind of questions Dillon was dealing with. But I've never quite figured out how you and Mr Hale fit in.'

Mrs Hale colored a little. 'Oh, Bob's on Dillon's board of directors. And since I was Bob's secretary for years in his own business, I just sat in and took notes.'

'Oh, of course. Thanks for telling me.' Heidi shook her hand. 'It's been a pleasure having you here. You're not leaving before breakfast, surely?'

'And give up my last chance to enjoy one of Kate's omelettes?' Mrs Hale laughed. 'Of course not.'

'But it's not the last chance, surely,' Heidi chided. 'Lilac Hill will always be here, just as it is today. We'd love to have you and Mr Hale come back to stay and really relax, whenever you can.'

Light footsteps sounded from the landing above them. Mrs Hale looked up, and Heidi followed her gaze re-

luctantly, for she'd recognized that step as Dillon's. He
was late this morning, and if she'd realized he wasn't
already in the dining-room Heidi wouldn't have been
hanging around the hall.

He paused on the stairway, one hand gracefully spread
across the wide walnut rail, and looked down at them
without a word. Today his suit was a silvery shade of
gray that made his hair and eyes look darker than usual.
But it wasn't his looks that held Heidi's attention so
strongly, and it wasn't the unspoken attraction which
lay between them, either—simple and devastating though
it was. Today, much as she would like to deny it, the
link was far deeper than mere attraction. She had faced
a great truth about herself last night, and it had not van-
ished in the light of morning. Just looking at Dillon
caused a kind of sensual ache.

What if she had gone to him last night? The question
echoed in her mind.

'That's very kind of you,' Mrs Hale said. She wasn't
even looking at Heidi, but at Dillon.

Heidi dragged her attention back to Mrs Hale. The
woman's neutral tone surprised her. Perhaps she'd been
pushing too hard for business, Heidi told herself. If
people were satisfied with their stay at Lilac Hill and
wanted to come back, they didn't need instructions. But
she couldn't seem to stop herself from adding, 'Just give
us a call and we'll make sure we have a room for you.'

Dillon moved, and Heidi looked up at him despite
herself. There was a gleam in his eyes which said he knew
perfectly well that she was babbling to cover up her own
sense of awkwardness.

'Don't forget to ask for the special rate,' Dillon murmured. 'Just mention my name; I'm sure that'll do it.'

Heidi glared at him.

Mrs Hale said, 'This week has been surprisingly relaxing, considering the amount of work that's been ac-

complished. I'm sure that's due to the wonderful surroundings and the lack of distractions.'

Dillon's eyes rested on Heidi. There was a tinge of irony in his gaze.

'You know, Dillon,' Mrs Hale added, 'it's not a bad idea to get certain special projects away from the pressure cooker of ordinary business. Not just for the Works, but for the other plants as well. It might increase production and creativity to the point it would be worth the monetary cost.'

'Lilac Hill as a sort of corporate retreat?' he said. 'That's a thought.'

'That's not exactly what I had in mind, though I'll bet you could keep this place booked full, Dillon.'

And then I could see him often, Heidi thought.

But something inside her made her shy away from the idea of any kind of exclusive contract; even if he could honestly keep Lilac Hill full with conferences and special projects, that sort of arrangement would make Heidi feel as if she was working for him—and that seemed strange and uncomfortable and not right. She couldn't flatly turn it down, though—not the business, and not the idea of seeing him.

'That's a great idea,' she said. 'We'd love to help—whenever the bed-and-breakfast trade leaves room.'

Dillon didn't comment, but Heidi sensed that he was watching her carefully as he followed her and Mrs Hale across to the dining-room, where Tweedledum and Tweedledee were just sitting down with loaded plates.

Kate stopped putting fresh French toast on the buffet and said tartly, 'That bacon's probably thawed by now, it's taken so long to get it.' She took the package out of Heidi's hand and gave her an empty plate instead.

So much for the idea of escaping, Heidi thought. She'd have to sit down across the table from Dillon and make a pretense of eating, at least.

Geneva pushed back her chair. 'Coffee, anyone?'

'Sit still, Mother, I'll get it.' Heidi set her unused plate back on the stack and picked up the coffee-pot.

Geneva sank back into her chair with an air of relief. She looked tired, Heidi thought guiltily. Well, that was nothing to wonder at. It had been a long week, with the house nearly full for the last few nights. And Heidi's picnic last night must have been the icing on the cake. Why had she been so selfish that she hadn't anticipated the strain that party would inevitably be on her mother?

Because the only thing I was thinking about was Dillon, she admitted.

Heidi stooped to press her cheek against Geneva's hair. 'Why don't you get a good rest today, dear?' she said softly. 'I have to stop at the bank after work, and I have some other errands to run, but I'll try to get home early to help Kate with the rooms.'

Geneva shook her head. 'I've got a conference this morning. Barry Evans' fiancée is coming with her mother to make arrangements for the engagement party. When she made the appointment, she asked about the wedding reception, too. Do you think we can handle that?'

Heidi frowned. She refilled her mother's cup, and moved on around the table to Mr Hale. Wedding receptions were a pain, she reminded herself, and they hadn't done enough of them yet to be really comfortable. This one was apt to be large, too, which multiplied the problems. But the money was good, and they weren't in any position to be turning down business.

'They're in a bit of a hurry to put everything together,' Geneva went on. 'The wedding's only six weeks off, so several places are booked already.' She seemed to remember her guests. 'But never mind, Heidi, we'll talk about it later.'

Heidi finished by topping off Mrs Hale's cup, and took the pot back to the sideboard. Dillon was still standing there, pouring syrup over his French toast. He asked, very softly, 'Barry Evans? Isn't he the one who called you the first night I was here? Are you disturbed that he's getting married?'

'Of course not,' Heidi said under her breath, and was annoyed when his eyebrows arched as if he didn't quite believe her. 'I'm disturbed that my mother forgot herself so much as to bring up business matters in front of guests.'

'That violates your rules?'

'Not mine. Hers.'

Dillon held a cup, and Heidi filled it. He looked over his shoulder at Geneva and said dispassionately, 'She looks tired. Is this getting to be too much for her?'

'She's worked awfully hard this week. We all have,' Heidi said defensively. They were all feeling the strain; Kate's temper was sharper than usual, and Heidi could hardly remember what day it was. It would be no wonder if Geneva looked as if she hadn't had enough sleep. It certainly didn't mean that the bed-and-breakfast business was getting to be too much for her.

'Then you'll be happy to get rid of us?' Dillon murmured.

'I didn't say that.'

'I'm glad.' The words were simple, but his tone made the phrase so intimate that it was almost a caress. 'And I'm glad to hear how you feel about Barry, too. I always did think he was the best illustration of your father's judgement.'

She stared at him, open-mouthed in shock. Dillon carried his plate to the table and sat down with the Hales. He plunged immediately into conversation, so Heidi couldn't ask what he'd meant. If Dillon had intended that comment as a compliment to Barry—and of course to George Cameron—then why had Barry been fired as one of the first actions of the new regime? And if he hadn't intended it as a compliment . . .

Of course he hadn't, she told herself. If he'd respected George Cameron, Dillon wouldn't have driven him out of business in the first place, would he?

Tweedledum and Tweedledee checked out on Friday afternoon, leaving only Dillon at Lilac Hill. Just like old times, Heidi thought as she made up the rooms for the new arrivals who would come for the weekend, remembering last week when Dillon had been their only guest. She reminded herself that the situation wouldn't continue long. Dillon hadn't yet said exactly when he'd be leaving, but it probably wouldn't be much longer. He'd said he would stay just long enough to take care of the loose ends—and how many loose ends could require his personal attention, anyway?

Better remember that, Heidi told herself. It would be much healthier for her state of mind if she didn't forget that he would be leaving. It would be so easy to let herself drift into thinking of the way she'd like things to be ...

She'd even dreamed last night—as she had often done in the months just after her father's death—of the easy pace of life as it used to be at Lilac Hill. She'd dreamed of a long autumn day, the air crisp and sweet as the apples which had grown on her favorite tree. And she'd seen herself as a little girl, picking flowers in the garden, while Geneva—in a flowing Victorian gown with a white parasol over her shoulder—walked out to the stable to visit her horses.

Heidi smiled a little at that; dreams were such silly things. Geneva had probably never owned a white parasol. And Heidi herself had without a doubt never been the charming, wistful and extraordinarily clean little girl of her dream. She'd have been gleefully pulling up weeds and flowers alike, in muddy handfuls.

At the end of her dream-day, they'd gathered as a family around the library fireplace, and the soft flicker of the flames had fallen across the beloved face of a man who sat in a leather wing-backed chair by the hearth and listened to his wife's description of the day as the little girl played at his feet...

That had been the end of her rest, and an abrupt one, too, for the dream had twisted as dreams often did, and Heidi had sat straight up in bed, stunned, clutching the sheet.

For the man in the wing-backed chair had not been her father, but Dillon. The girl-child had looked like him, with her dark hair in long, glossy curls. And Heidi herself had been there, but not playing in front of the fire where she'd expected to be. She'd been sitting in the matching wing-backed chair instead, telling the man she loved about her day...

She had cried then, as she admitted what she had not been able to acknowledge openly before. Her attraction to Dillon Archer was a whole lot more than simple sensuality. She was in love with him.

The confession came as no real surprise; somewhere deep inside her she had faced the truth long ago, but simply refused to admit it openly. And while she'd hidden the facts from herself her love had slowly grown and flowered until now there was no weeding it out of her heart.

No matter what he'd done—no matter how severely his actions had affected her life, and Geneva's, and her father's—she loved him, and she would love him always.

'I want to be his wife,' she whispered painfully.

No wonder that this morning when Mrs Hale had made her suggestion about the future of Lilac Hill Heidi had shied away from the very idea of working for him. To be his employee, when she wanted so very much more...

'I want forever,' she admitted out loud.

But forever was precisely what she couldn't have. Her dream was faded and threadbare now as cool daylight intruded. The long autumn days she had pictured with such pleasure were filled with work. The horses and the favorite apple tree were gone, never to return. And as for the image of Dillon by the fire...

She could have nothing at all, or she could have the bare bones of her dream. Those were her only options. She could not have the dream itself.

But to accept the skeleton without the substance was to make a mockery of everything she wanted. And so she would choose to have nothing.

And for the rest of his stay she would treat him as she treated any other guest—as one among many who would come into her life and soon depart—leaving ripples perhaps, and memories, but nothing which would really change the pattern of her days.

It didn't work, of course. For one thing, the new arrivals came and settled into their rooms and then went off to dinner and their own pursuits, while Dillon came back from the Works and accepted Geneva's invitation to join them for pot roast. It was difficult to slot him in with the others when he behaved so naturally as if he belonged at Lilac Hill.

How quickly he had fitted into the pattern of their lives! He automatically plumped the cushion at Geneva's back before she sat down in the library for a drink before dinner. And he didn't ask what Heidi wanted, just poured her usual small sherry and brought it to her.

He didn't say a word to her, however. He didn't have to, for the air between them seemed to throb, and idle conversation would have been no more than a game. And when he strolled across the room to look at a book which had caught his attention, Heidi's gaze followed him hungrily, despite all her efforts to ignore him. Just watching him move was a treat, and also a temptation.

How had she managed to convince herself that it was even worth a try to think about him as she would any other guest? It was a plan doomed to failure, and if she'd had any sense she wouldn't have tried to fool herself.

Heidi was very quiet during dinner, hardly paying attention to the conversation between her mother and Dillon. Afterwards, she chose a quiet corner of the drawing-room and drank her coffee. Occasionally Geneva cast a worried look at her, but she didn't push for an explanation of Heidi's unnatural silence. Dillon, who seemed willing to give her all the time in the world to think, kept his distance—but the way he looked at her now and then was enough to keep her heart pounding and her mind in turmoil.

The other guests trickled slowly back from their evening out, and the drawing-room came to life with laughter and stories. Almost all the guest rooms would be full once more, and tonight there seemed to be no wallflowers, no one needing to be drawn out and made to feel comfortable. Heidi was grateful for that, and before ten o'clock she stooped over her mother's chair and said softly, 'If you don't need me, darling, I'm going to bed. I've got a ghastly headache.'

Geneva's brows drew together in concern, but she only nodded and turned her attention back to the guest she'd been talking to.'

Heidi hadn't been lying; her head did ache. But it wasn't the sort of pain which aspirin and rest would cure. So she didn't go to bed; instead she went to the kitchen—deserted now that Kate had loaded the dishwasher and gone out to her own quarters—to pick up the mail. She could at least sort out the new bills and answer the letters requesting information or reservations.

She was on her way back to the main hall when she saw Dillon come quietly in from the back terrace with an armload of logs and turn toward the stairs. The lights had been dimmed, and the wall sconces threw long shadows that wheeled around the room as he moved. He was going up to his room to enjoy some solitude, she concluded, and drew back a little into the darkness of a doorway. But he saw her move, and he paused at the foot of the staircase.

It was obviously too late to retreat, so Heidi joined him.

'Bored with all the companionship?' he said.

She shrugged. 'It gets a little dull sometimes. Bed-and-breakfast is a lot chummier than the average hotel. Are you getting tired of it?'

Dillon's eyes were brilliant, despite the soft lighting, and she could feel the warmth of his gaze as he studied her. If he had been running his hands over her face, sketching each feature with his fingertips, it could not have been any more intimate a touch.

'Not all of it,' he said. 'If you'd like to join me...'

She looked down at the mail she held, trying to hide the confusion she felt. She had to stifle a shiver, caused not by cold unpleasantness but by the electrical thrill of that almost physical touch, and the desire that bubbled up inside her.

You've made this decision once, she reminded herself, and shook her head.

He didn't press her. At the landing, he simply said goodnight and went down the hall to the oriole suite, while Heidi climbed the steps to the playroom and sat flipping through the mail without paying attention to a single bit of it.

She should be glad that the incident had passed without unpleasantness, she told herself. She should be... but she wasn't.

Her mind was playing games, picturing him down in the room which used to be hers, kneeling in front of the hearth to build a fire. A fire she could share, if she chose to go down and knock on his door...

And it was her choice—entirely her choice. Dillon had used seductive kisses, and sensual tricks, and all the persuasion at his command, but he had not used force. He'd

had the power to do so—or at least to make a good try—
but he hadn't blackmailed her after all.

She sat at her desk, toying with the letter-opener, and
thought about it. If he had pressed her, she might well
have taken him up on his bargain. A bargain, she reminded herself, that would have been nothing of the
sort—Dillon had intended to keep the Works open no
matter what she did. So he'd had nothing to lose by delaying his announcement.

Instead, he had sacrificed the advantage he'd held
rather than push her. Surely that said he wasn't the
heartless, soulless creature she'd originally thought he
was.

Perhaps her mother was right. If Geneva could forgive,
and enjoy his companionship as she so obviously did,
perhaps it was time for Heidi as well to let bygones be
bygones.

But if all she could have was a little time, and not the
forever she dreamed of...

Then she'd take it, Heidi decided, and be grateful for
it. And she wouldn't look back or dream of what might
have been.

Without another thought, she started down the stairs
to go to him. Then a laughing group of guests came up
to the landing on their way to their rooms, and Heidi
ducked back up to the playroom. She couldn't afford to
be seen slipping into his room, that was for sure. What
had happened to her brain?

She waited a little longer, nerves stretched to the limit
now that she'd finally made up her mind, wondering
when she would be sure that she'd be undetected.

Eventually Geneva came upstairs. 'How's your head,
dear?'

'Better. But I might go down and get some warm milk
after a while.'

'I've got aspirin if you need some.'

'No, thanks, Mom.' She felt like a hypocrite when Geneva kissed her tenderly and went on into her room.

Heidi finished opening the mail while she waited for the house to quiet. At least the action kept her hands busy. Nothing, right now, could quiet her mind.

The letter from the bank was at the very bottom of the pile, and Heidi almost dismissed it as just another piece of advertising. Then she realized it was not a form letter, for the address was individually typed. And it was not part of a mailing to all customers, for it bore a first-class stamp.

There had been a time when a personal letter from a bank wouldn't have bothered her; George Cameron had been on the boards of several, and bankers had numbered among the family friends for years. But now Heidi had experience with occasional cash flow shortages and even the once-in-a-while overdraft. And these days she knew that personal letters from bankers were usually not invitations to tea.

But she couldn't think what it might be about. She'd paid the mortgage yesterday, on the precise day it was due. The regular payment on their business loan wasn't due for two more weeks. She'd deposited all the cash Dillon had given her in the last week, so surely her balance was still adequate.

She opened the envelope with trepidation. A slip of paper slid out and fluttered to the floor, and she recognized the check she'd written to cover the mortgage payment.

She gave a little sigh of combined relief and frustration. She'd probably forgotten to sign it, or botched up the numbers—heaven knew she'd been barely functioning when she'd written that check, right before the picnic had started. The bank must be returning it for further attention. It was a nuisance, of course, and she'd probably have to add a penalty for making her payment late instead of on the proper day, but——

There was nothing wrong with the check. It was clearly written, the numbers printed plainly and without mistake, and the signature was textbook perfect. Which made sense; if there had been an error, why wouldn't the teller have caught it yesterday when she'd made the payment?

Heidi unfolded the letter. It was short and to the point, and merely said that the teller who had taken her payment had been in error, because the bank no longer held the mortgage on Lilac Hill. It had been sold, as was allowed under the agreement Geneva had signed.

'Sold,' she said under her breath, almost unaware that she'd spoken.

The sale had been so recent, the letter went on, that the paperwork had not quite all been processed, and so the bank had not sent the appropriate notices yet. In the near future, of course, Geneva would be receiving all the paperwork, and instructions from the new owner of the mortgage as to how to make future payments. And the new owner of the mortgage was...

Heidi dropped the letter on her desk and buried her face in her hands. Dillon, of course. It was right there before her in black and white, and still she couldn't bring herself to accept that it was true. She had to blink hard and look again before she could be sure.

What was it Callie had teased her about one day? Something about Dillon's not being satisfied with the Works, but wanting the rest of the Cameron empire as well. And when Heidi had said there wasn't much left of the Cameron empire, Callie had pointed out, 'There's Lilac Hill... And there's you.'

Suddenly it looked as if he intended to go after both— as if he thought they were some kind of package deal.

CHAPTER TEN

DILLON had said he wouldn't blackmail her over the Works, but he hadn't made any promises about other forms of force.

Heidi hadn't realized before how carefully that promise had been phrased, but now the memory rang hollowly in her mind of the precise words he had used. 'I wouldn't blackmail you over the Works,' he'd said. 'Because, you see, I don't have to.'

But now he had a different kind of carrot to tempt her with—one she could not turn her back on lightly. Her home . . . her mother's home. If he was to tell Heidi that she was the price for Lilac Hill . . .

Heidi didn't know, of course, that he'd do anything of the sort—but she had little confidence that he wouldn't. She'd thought all along that it was unlike him to back away from such a tempting bargain as the Works offered—one which would cost him nothing, one which had been dropped in his lap almost by providence. History said he wouldn't hesitate to take what he wanted, no matter what means were necessary to bring it within reach—except, perhaps, when his business was at stake. So he'd chosen to make his announcement, and he'd simply taken another route to get what he wanted. And if in the meantime he'd managed to keep Heidi off guard, and off balance, he'd probably considered that an advantage . . .

It had almost worked, she thought. She had almost gone to him in love.

The house was almost quiet as Heidi crept down the stairs. A television set murmured from the sandpiper suite, but there was no other sound. She hesitated before knocking on the door of the oriole suite, for she couldn't hear even the crackle of a flame. If Dillon had doused the fire and gone to bed . . . Perhaps she would wait until tomorrow.

But she didn't want to wait, to face him over the breakfast table and wonder what new plot lay behind the smile. And there would be no privacy then for a confrontation.

Dillon opened the door, and for a moment the sheer disbelief which shone in his eyes made Heidi pause in doubt. Then he drew her inside, and closed the door, and without a word cupped her face in his hands and kissed her long and hungrily.

It wasn't fair, she thought, that even when she knew what was in his mind all he had to do was touch her—look at her—and she reacted like ice-cream on a hot day.

He kissed her once more, softly, and drew her over to the *chaise-longue* by the fire. The room was dark, except for the last flicker of the flames. He had been sitting on the *chaise*—the cushions were crumpled—with his tie off and the sleeves of his white shirt rolled up to the elbow. Very gently he eased her on to the *chaise-longue* and settled beside her.

The reality was different from her dream, of course, but it was close enough to tug at her heart. The two of them, together . . .

Heidi couldn't help thinking of how different this would be right now if only she hadn't read the mail. She would have come down here to love him, without a hint of hesitation in her heart. But as it was . . .

He whispered her name, and his voice, husky with desire, made her ache with an answering longing.

She still wanted him. Overwhelmingly, without limits, without reason; she wanted him so much that she was about to forget everything and make love with him anyway. Perhaps, she thought, if she pretended hard enough that he cared about her too, she could convince herself that someday there would be more between them than simple desire ...

The last fragment of common sense made her ask, But when all is said and done, what will you have except a threadbare dream? Certainly it won't be the love you want to share.

He whispered against her lips, 'I knew you couldn't deny this, Heidi.'

For a moment longer she held to the illusion, and then she pushed it resolutely away, and said, very deliberately, 'And you tried to make sure of it, didn't you, Dillon?'

He drew back a little, and frowned, but he didn't let her go.

For the first time Heidi paused to think of the situation she had gotten herself into. Not only was she alone with him in a sleeping house, half lying on a *chaise-longue*, but she had come into his room of her own accord. And it must seem as if she had gone quite willingly into his embrace, for she had made no effort to keep him from kissing her. If he called her a tease, he would be more than justified. And if he tried to hold her here against her will——

Heidi put both hands against his chest and pushed. His arms tightened around her, making her feel tiny and helpless and utterly powerless in his grip. Her fingertips tingled from the contact, and through the silk of his shirt she could feel the heavy beat of his heart. Was it pounding so because of desire, or anger, or some combination which might be even more combustible than either emotion alone?

'What are you talking about? I didn't exactly drag you in here.' Dillon's voice had a rough edge that frightened her.

'No. You said you wouldn't use the Works to blackmail me.'

His eyes narrowed warily. They looked like black slits in the uneven light, but Heidi would swear that for an instant she had seen a glint of wry humor. 'And you're holding that against me?'

'But you'll admit you started out to use blackmail?'

'You presented me with a perfect opportunity, that's sure.'

Heidi had to admit that was true. She'd walked straight into the trap, even though she hadn't been the one who designed it. But there wasn't much point in arguing just now about precisely what had inspired the idea. 'You threatened me,' she said. 'And you thought the matter through very carefully before you changed your mind. Why, Dillon? Were you concerned that it wouldn't work after all? Or had you found a surer way to put pressure on me?'

'I don't know what you're talking about, Heidi.'

'Oh, don't play games. I know about the mortgage, you see.'

This time, when she pushed, his grip loosened. Heidi was grimly pleased that she had startled him with that bit of information. She slid away from him and off the *chaise-longue* to stand before the fire. 'You didn't expect me to know about that yet, did you?'

'The mortgage has nothing to do with this, Heidi.'

'Only because you were keeping it as a last resort.' She held out her hands to the dying flames; even though the trembling of her fingers was not due to cold, the heat felt soothing. 'I suppose I should be flattered that you want me badly enough to go to such lengths.'

'Don't be,' he said. His voice was grim.

She turned her head to look at him then. 'I see. You won't be happy till you've mopped up everything the Camerons ever had, not only the Works but Lilac Hill as well. I'm just incidental—is that it?'

He didn't bother to answer. Heidi turned finally to face him. He was sitting at the end of the *chaise-longue*, arms folded across his chest, staring at the flames as if he was looking into oblivion. She had never seen the lines of his face look so hard, like a marble sculpture.

'What made you hate my father so much?' she whispered. 'You took his customers, and ruined his business. Now you want Lilac Hill. And me—as some sort of appetizer, I suppose.'

'Damn it, Heidi, I told you what happened to the Works was normal business competition. And as for you and Lilac Hill——' He stopped, as if for once he didn't have an easy explanation on the tip of his tongue.

'You won't settle till you have it all, will you, Dillon? What did my father ever do to you to make you so vengeful that you took his business, and his life—and even then you're not satisfied?'

He looked at her then. *'What did you say?'*

Heidi's voice was almost gentle. 'I said you caused the heart attack that killed him.'

His face was a frozen mask.

'I don't think you understood where the pressure you put on him would lead, but the result was the same, wasn't it?'

Dillon jumped up. In the shifting patterns of the firelight, he looked taller and even more dangerous. 'I suppose I should be grateful you're acquitting me of premeditated murder!'

Heidi shrank back a step. He was between her and the door; how had she been foolish enough to let that happen?

But he didn't come toward her; he stood by the fireplace instead, with his hands braced on the mantel, his back to her.

After a moment, Heidi asked, 'Why are you keeping the Works open, Dillon? Does your conscience bother you?'

His voice had an edge as dangerous as sharpened steel. 'Of course not. You know very well I haven't one.' He turned to face her. 'So you honestly think I bought the mortgage on Lilac Hill because I want you so badly I'd do anything to get you?'

'Didn't you?'

He didn't answer. Instead he smiled just a little—not at all a humorous smile—and took a step toward her. 'Well, if that's the case, why should I stop at blackmail, Heidi? Why not force?'

Heidi shuddered away from him, but she wasn't quick enough. Dillon seized her shoulders; his fingers dug into her muscles with pitiless strength, and he stared down into her eyes for a moment that seemed to stretch into forever.

'I'll scream.' Even as she said it, Heidi knew how stupid it must sound—threatening to scream, when her throat was so tight with panic that she could do no more than whisper.

The dark eyes flickered with contempt. 'You could have done that long ago—but you didn't. And you wouldn't.'

He pushed her away; Heidi stumbled and caught herself against the edge of the *chaise-longue*.

'Well, you're wrong about my motives,' he said. 'And you have an inflated notion of your value, too. I don't want you nearly that much.'

She was in the clear, almost at the door, but something stopped her from running. 'Then why did you buy the mortgage, Dillon?'

'Because Mrs Hale's idea of a corporate retreat sounded too good to pass by.' He rubbed his temples as if his head hurt. 'And when Lilac Hill goes under, as it surely will—because you've got no more business sense than your father did—I'll be waiting.'

Heidi turned on her heel and marched out. She would not stand there and listen to him insult her father.

But her feet dragged as she climbed the steps to her own room once more. She ought to feel satisfaction—

she had certainly been successful in getting her point across. But it hadn't turned out as she'd expected. Why had she not anticipated that Dillon might still have some threats of his own?

'When Lilac Hill goes under, as it surely will'...

Well, it wouldn't. She'd show Dillon Archer, even if she had to work day and night and take yet another job to make ends meet. She would not surrender to threats, to blackmail, to force. She would not give in, no matter what he did.

She started to shiver uncontrollably as she remembered the way he had held her by the shoulders, helpless in his grip. How easy it would have been for him to subdue her! Lilac Hill was not so sturdily built that a scream would go unheard, but she had been incapable of screaming, and Dillon had known it.

How foolhardy could she be? Why had she even gone down to his room tonight? What had possessed her to take the chance? What had she thought she would accomplish, anyway, that was worth putting herself into the grip of a man capable of the things he had done, the things he had threatened to do...?

Realization hit her, as sudden and blinding as lightning stabbing through the dark night sky. She had gone because she'd believed he'd never do such a thing. Because she had known, deep inside her heart, that he'd been half teasing all the time, that he'd never carry out those threats.

But that was ridiculous...

Or was it? He'd almost come straight out and said, once, that he hadn't taken it seriously himself. When he'd told her that he would never blackmail her over the Works, he'd added, almost under his breath, 'No matter how much fun it is to think about'...

And so she had gone to him tonight secure in her belief that no matter what she said or did she would be safe.

Even as she had flung her accusations at him, she had been certain she could trust him not to hurt her.

Staggered by the enormity of that knowledge, she flung herself down on her bed.

She hadn't been quite correct, of course. Her shoulders ached from his grip, and her self-esteem felt as full of holes as Swiss cheese. But in essence her half-conscious conviction had been right.

And what did that tell her about Dillon Archer—the man who saw what he wanted and went after it, no matter what the cost to others?

One thing was certain, she reflected. He had been telling the truth, there at the end, when he'd said he didn't want Heidi enough to spend a cent to coerce her.

Few of the guests were stirring yet on Saturday morning when Heidi came down. Kate was already in the kitchen, of course. Her famous blueberry muffins were on the menu today, and the first pan was just coming out of the oven when Heidi appeared. Normally she would have snatched one, as much to tease Kate as to appease her hunger. This time, without a word, she piled all twelve in a basket and carried it to the dining-room buffet.

When she came back, Kate was looking at her with an odd expression. Heidi braced herself for questions; her almost sleepless night was undoubtedly written on her face.

But Kate said only, 'If you want to be really helpful, you can start the scrambled eggs. I expect with the crowd we've got we'll need at least half a gallon of them this morning.'

Kitchen duty sounded just fine to Heidi. The last thing she wanted was to face Dillon in front of a roomful of strangers. She really didn't want to face him at all, but of course total avoidance wasn't an option. So long as he stayed at Lilac Hill—and she had no doubt he'd stay just as long as it was convenient for him, no matter whether he was wanted or not—she'd simply have to adjust herself to reality. She'd have to be frigidly polite to him, and hope Geneva and Kate wouldn't ask too many questions.

She scrambled eggs till she thought her arm would fall off from stirring, and made piles of link sausage and toast. The breakfast rush seemed to go on forever. When it was finally over, Heidi turned on the dishwasher, put to soak the plates which had to wait for the next load, and poured herself a cup of coffee. 'How do you do this every day?' she sighed as she sank down at the kitchen table to rest.

Kate looked down at her, brow furrowed. 'I just do what's next on the list without thinking much about it. And what's next on the list right now is the rooms. We might as well start.'

Heidi said, 'Surely people haven't left for the day yet.' She kept her tone casual, hoping that Kate would say Dillon, at least, had eaten his breakfast and gone off to town.

'Probably not. Most of the rooms will have to wait. But we can turn the oriole suite out completely this morning while we're waiting for everyone else to get off to their day's activities.'

Heidi heard her own shocked gasp. Her heart seemed to sink to her heels. The oriole suite... he was gone, then. And he didn't intend to come back.

Kate nodded solemnly. 'I had a feeling you didn't know that. He left at daylight—took a cup of coffee with him and was on his way. He said to tell your mother he'd be in touch about the balance on his bill.'

Heidi said, almost automatically, 'There isn't one. Not really.'

'Which is it?' Kate asked shrewdly. 'Either he's paid up or he isn't.'

Heidi wasn't paying any attention. Even if she dared charge him for the rest of his stay, she'd no doubt have a heck of a time collecting the money. 'When Lilac Hill goes under, as it surely will'... He'd probably take pleasure in being part of that cash-flow crunch.

'And he said to tell you——'

Heidi's gaze flew to Kate's face. If he'd left her a message...

'—that he'd send the coffee-cup he took this morning back to you as soon as he was done with it. He seemed to think you'd be worried about it.'

There was half-conscious mimicry in Kate's voice, and Heidi had no trouble figuring out exactly the sarcastic tone in which Dillon had said it. 'Good,' she said briskly. 'I'd hate to break up a set of china for his sake. Let's get started, Kate.'

The sooner his presence was wiped out of Lilac Hill, she thought, the better.

Cleaning the room was easy. Destroying the memories of him was not. Geneva was particularly unhappy with the suddenness of Dillon's departure. 'But what did he *say*?' she asked Kate in a bewildered tone, when she was given the news. Heidi, who couldn't bear to hear the answer again, mumbled something about an errand and took herself off.

It was four days before the letter came. It was waiting on the kitchen table when Heidi and Geneva came back from an afternoon of shopping, and Geneva pounced on it as if it had been gold. Heidi barely got a glimpse, but it was enough to see that the envelope was fine ivory stationery with the return address of Archer Enterprises engraved on the corner. And she could tell from the slimness of the envelope that the letter inside was a single page, or maybe two—but no more.

Geneva carried it into the library with her. Heidi waited for a couple of minutes, biting her lip, and then went to fix her mother a cup of tea. She suspected Geneva might need it.

When Heidi came into the library a little later, Geneva was sitting in her favorite chair, dabbing the corners of her eyes with a hanky. Heidi almost dumped the tray she carried in her haste to get to her mother's side.

'Don't be silly,' Geneva said. 'It's not bad news... It's just that he's not coming back for a while.'

Then he would be coming back? But of course he would return; he still owned the Works, and it would need his attention from time to time. There was no reason to panic—and there was certainly no cause for relief, either.

Geneva looked down at the letter lying open in her lap and dabbed at her eyes again. 'Oh, Heidi, he's paid off the mortgage on Lilac Hill.'

'He's bought it, Mother. It's a whole different thing. It doesn't mean we don't still owe the money, we just have to pay Dillon instead of the bank.'

'No,' Geneva said. 'It's right here—he says, "Don't concern yourself about making further payments."'

Heidi picked up the ivory letterhead. Geneva was right, as far as she'd gone. But the next sentence read, 'It's taken care of for the present.'

For the present? It didn't take a genius to figure out what that meant. He wasn't giving up the mortgage, just suspending payments, so someday—perhaps when Geneva was no longer in the picture—there would be a reckoning. Heidi already knew who would come out on the short end of that settlement. Dillon had it all planned...

Heidi frowned. But it didn't make sense, she thought. If he believed the bed-and-breakfast was doomed, and he was waiting eagerly to get his hands on Lilac Hill, why had he taken a great deal of the pressure off by relieving them of mortgage payments?

Blood money, she thought, and wasn't aware she'd said it aloud till Geneva repeated the words.

'Blood money? What do you mean, dear?'

'I mean he feels sorry about what he did to you, Mother.'

'I think it's sweet of him to be concerned, but——'

'Sweet? Mother, it's his fault there's a mortgage on Lilac Hill at all! I suppose it should be a relief to know the man does have a conscience, no matter what he says, but after what he did to this family——'

'Heidi!' Geneva sounded appalled. 'I don't know the whole story of what went on a couple of years ago between Dillon and your father. George was never one to take me into his confidence where business was concerned. But as I've gotten to know Dillon, I can't believe he was cruel, or even unethical—it's not in his nature.'

'Mother——'

'And if you can't see Dillon any more clearly than that—if you don't recognize simple generosity when you see it...' Geneva shook her head and held out a folded slip of paper. 'Here's his check for what he estimates is the balance of his bill. And as for the rest, I'd suggest you think this over very carefully, Heidi, before you do something you'll always regret.'

She went out, and the hush of the library settled around Heidi once more. But it wasn't a comforting silence this time. She hadn't been so thoroughly scolded since she was a child, and Geneva's words stung like alcohol on a broken blister. It wasn't fair that her mother was taking Dillon's side, defending him, making him out to be some kind of saint. After all they'd been through, because of him...

And as for saying his actions came out of simple generosity... what did her mother know about Dillon's motives? Geneva was mistaken, that was all.

Or did she understand something that Heidi wouldn't let herself see, even now?

Heidi unfolded the check and eyed the figures and the firm black signature. Over the weekend, out of sheer pique, she'd added up the totals and figured out what

Dillon had promised but not yet paid. The check was for more than that; his estimates had erred on the generous side——

Generous. There was that word again.

He probably didn't intend to be generous, she told herself. He'd no doubt meant it as some kind of grandstand gesture, proving to Heidi that he could buy and sell the Camerons any time he chose...

But he didn't owe them a cent. Whether the price he'd paid for the Works was a fair one or not was beyond Heidi's power to know, but she was forced to admit that George Cameron had agreed to it, and therefore Dillon was under no further obligation. He'd stuck to the original bargain for the price of his room, even after Heidi had confessed her scheme to cheat him. He'd certainly not been obliged to pay for the party she'd arranged—but he had. The money was in her hands this moment. And in matters where money wasn't concerned—like the afternoon he'd spent sawing up that fallen tree—he'd been generous as well. He'd even taken it upon himself, when he'd got that odd letter from George Cameron's old friend, to break the news of George's death himself, so that Geneva didn't have to.

All right, she admitted. What Geneva called simple generosity was a part of him; Heidi couldn't keep on denying it completely. But so was the part of him that had ruined the Works.

'That was normal business competition', he had said. And now he was rebuilding it...

Only because he'd figured out a way to profit. What was it Masters had said about that? Dillon would find a way to make a profit in any circumstances, that was it.

So where was the profit for him in buying up a considerable mortgage, and forgiving payments?

He's got an angle figured out for the future, Heidi told herself. Or maybe he had only Geneva in mind; since the first day he'd come to Lilac Hill he'd seemed to pay special attention to her comfort and well-being. He'd seemed to be always there to plump the cushion at her back, to hold her chair, to notice when she was tired. It was possible, Heidi supposed, that he was being generous—intending to relieve Geneva's mind by taking care of the mortgage. It was her house, after all. And it was his fault the mortgage existed.

And where did that leave Heidi?

Just squarely nowhere, she told herself. But was there anything to be surprised at in that?

She had judged him very harshly, in her anger and frustration. She had desperately wanted him to love her for herself, and so when she had seen what she'd thought was evidence of his cold calculation she had reacted before she'd stopped to think. She had lashed out at him in self-protection, sacrificing the chance to have anything at all, because she had been afraid it would not be enough to satisfy her. Because she had known in the secret depths of her heart that if she'd once slept with him she would have been lost, drowning in her love for a man who didn't care about her.

Unconsciously, she ran a fingertip across his signature, caressing the paper as if it had been his skin. When she caught herself doing it, she smiled bitterly, and folded the check away.

Geneva was right about one thing—Heidi not only regretted what she had done, but she would always regret it. She had no option but to regret, for there would be no fixing it now.

CHAPTER ELEVEN

A MONTH rolled by. Mitch was out of town again on another prospecting trip when the city council met in closed session and refused to grant Masters any of the extra concessions he wanted in order to build his plant.

If Heidi hadn't known better, she'd have suspected Mitch had foreseen the vote and scheduled his trip on purpose so that he could leave her to deal with Masters. The chicken tycoon, who had come back to town to make his case, was spitting mad over the refusal, and he threatened to call a press conference to make sure Fairview's citizens knew how irresponsible their elected officials were in refusing to co-operate with a business which could have such a positive impact on the city.

Heidi managed to derail his intention only by reminding him that a public forum would make him miss the day's last flight, and she delivered him to the airport with a sigh of relief.

To think she had once believed that if Masters bought the Works he'd be an improvement over Dillon!

But that line of thought brought only heartache, and so she turned back to her work with more determination than enthusiasm. Nothing was as simple as it had been before Dillon came—the Ambassadors' job seemed suddenly to be mere paper-shuffling, and as for the bed-and-breakfast trade...

If she was honest, she had to admit she was tired of her home being filled with strangers. That was on top of the fact that most of the time she was just plain exhausted from all the work.

And she was a bit depressed as well. She needed to say a few things to Dillon, whether he wanted to hear them or not. But it seemed there wasn't to be an opportunity. A whole month, and there hadn't been a word from him except for the letter to Geneva, and the check Heidi had no intention of cashing. He hadn't even fulfilled his promise to send back the coffee-cup he'd taken with him that last morning.

One Friday she had lunch with Callie Martin, who said frankly, 'You look ghastly, Heidi. You aren't regretting Barry's wedding after all, are you?'

That, Heidi thought, was the final straw. People were going to start asking questions. It would be bad enough if they settled on Barry as the explanation for her strange behavior—but a whole lot worse if they went one step further...

She was simply going to have to pull herself together and stop waiting for Dillon to come back. If there was no other way, she'd write him a letter.

But she shied away from that, for the only address she had was a business one, and she didn't want her apology to go through the hands of a secretary. Still, if that was the only choice...

She was thinking about how she could word her letter when she came back to the Ambassadors' office after lunch. The secretary looked up from the mail she was opening and said, 'The Works just called. There's to be a major announcement in half an hour.'

'Nice notice,' Heidi muttered.

'You got the same warning the Press did,' Betty pointed out as she turned back to the mail.

A press conference at any of the major businesses called for someone from the Ambassadors to be present. Since Mitch was still gone, that meant it would have to be Heidi who went.

'You may get your chance after all,' she muttered as she drove across town. But she tried to concentrate on the event rather than think about the odds of Dillon's being there.

What constituted a major announcement, anyway? Maybe it was just a matter of a few new job openings. That could be considered major, in the circumstances—but Dillon wasn't likely to be present for something of that nature.

But she saw his Jaguar as she parked in the company lot, and she took a few deep breaths to try to calm herself before she buzzed the receptionist at the main entrance and was admitted.

She was almost late, and the largest conference-room was already filled with people. She recognized a couple of reporters from the newspaper, and a crew from the local television station was waiting, cameras already set up. The conference table had been pushed to one end of the room and several chairs were lined up behind it.

Sitting on the table, one foot swinging, chatting with the onlookers without, apparently, a care in the world, was Dillon.

He didn't even look up when Heidi came in.

She told herself drily, There goes another illusion. She'd been convinced that there was a link of awareness between them—she'd felt it so strongly herself that she'd been positive he must feel it too. But she'd been wrong, for if that awareness had ever existed except in her own mind surely he couldn't be oblivious to her presence now.

And he was certainly oblivious. Even when he scanned the crowd, his gaze didn't hesitate as it swept over her.

But she couldn't stop herself from drinking in the sight of him. He looked magnificent in a dark blue suit, a little more formal than she had seen him wear before. Or did the formality lie in his manner instead? Despite his casual pose, there was a sternness about him that was unfamiliar.

In response to some unseen signal, several people took seats behind the table, and Dillon moved to the podium and began to read from a prepared text.

Heidi tried to concentrate on his words, though just hearing his voice was enough to shake her self-control. She picked up enough fragments, however, to know that this was the biggest thing Fairview had seen in years. There would be an enlargement of the factory and renovation of several buildings to allow the manufacture of not only the crates and boxes and bubbles and pouches they had always made but of the machinery which would automatically pack a customer's products inside those protective devices. It was a whole new kind of process— and it would provide a great many new jobs. Highly skilled jobs, at that, and well-paid ones.

The reaction was as overwhelming as anyone could have hoped. Heidi waited till the rush had died down somewhat before she made her way to the front of the room, but there were still a number of people about, and she had to raise her voice. 'Dillon, I'm so glad. This will be wonderful for Fairview.'

Dillon shrugged. 'I was going to do it somewhere. It just happened to be here.'

Heidi felt as if she'd been slapped. 'Of course,' she agreed in a brittle tone. 'I'm sorry if it sounded as if I was trying to take personal credit!'

His eyes were dark and disturbing.

You didn't come here to quarrel with him all over again, Heidi reminded herself. 'Look, I'm sorry for lots of things,' she said quietly.

His gaze flickered, and his voice was soft. 'I said a few things I shouldn't have, too.'

For an endless moment Heidi stood there frozen, her hopes rising insanely, and then someone called for his attention and Dillon said, 'I'll be with you in a minute.' He didn't take his gaze off Heidi's face, but one dark eyebrow quirked as if to inquire why she was monopolizing him.

Her mood plummeted even more rapidly than it had risen. What a fool she was to read anything into that careless apology! She smiled with an effort. 'Then we'll call it quits and forget it ever happened. I won't keep you, Dillon, but there's one more thing—Mother would love to see you, I know.'

He nodded. 'I'll stop by to visit her late this afternoon. If it's not inconvenient for you, that is.'

'No... Not at all.'

'I'm staying at the hotel.'

'Of course.' She held out a hand, hoping her fingers wouldn't tremble and betray her. 'I'll be seeing you around town, then. Best wishes, Dillon.'

He nodded and pressed her hand for a moment, and then Heidi turned away and walked out.

It was one of the most difficult things she had ever done.

Heidi tried to manufacture errands to keep her away from Lilac Hill till after he would have come and gone, but fate was against her. She'd never had such a smooth and easy time at the bank, the library, the gas station. And so she was home earlier than she'd wanted to be.

But the Jaguar was not parked behind the house, as she'd half expected it would be, and Geneva said she hadn't seen Dillon at all.

'I'm going for a walk,' Heidi said, and when Geneva frowned she added quickly, 'He's coming to see you, Mother, not me. But you might give him back his check, and tell him his account is more than paid up.'

Geneva nodded and added drily, 'Do you want me to hang a towel out the attic window when it's safe for you to come back to the house?'

'Mother, don't you dare——'

'All right, I won't say anything to Dillon. But you're being silly.'

It all looked so simple to Geneva, Heidi thought wryly as she wandered along the obscure little trails she had known since childhood. But then Geneva didn't know how stupid Heidi had been.

She reached the little clearing where they'd shared a picnic breakfast, and where they'd had their first quarrel, and sat down on a log to watch the sunlight gleaming like jewels on the rippling water. She had accused him that day of purposely destroying her father's business, and he hadn't quite denied it; he'd said it was only competition.

What if she had told him then that she blamed him for George Cameron's death as well? Would he have passed that off as something which he'd had no control over? Or would she simply have faced that black anger sooner? Would he have walked away then, and left her alone?

Not that it would have made any real difference, she concluded. Long before that day in the clearing she'd been in love with him.

She dug in the pocket of her jeans for a tissue and blew her nose. A lot of good it was going to do, sitting here feeling sorry for herself!

She didn't hear footsteps. She didn't hear anything until Dillon was almost beside her. 'You've been crying,' he said.

Heidi didn't look at him. She stared at the little stream and lied. 'I have hay fever. I'm always like this in the late summer.'

'Oh.' He put his hands in the pockets of his chinos and stood looking down at her. 'Your mother said you went for a walk, so I thought I might find you here.'

'I told you a long time ago, it's one of my favorite places.' And I didn't choose to come here because of memories of you, she wanted to add defiantly.

'So you did. I came out here to tell you I can't just forget it all happened, Heidi, as you suggested we do.'

'You might as well. It wasn't important.'

'Wasn't it?'

'No.' She fumbled for her tissue again. The silence lengthened till she couldn't stand it any more, for each instant lent more weight, more importance, to the question. She had to do something to break the tension.

Finally she managed to laugh, and said, 'Oh, I was silly enough to think it was, at the time. You can be pretty intense, you know that?'

He didn't speak, and she dared to look up at him through her lashes. His eyes were dark and full of incredulity, and Heidi's heart seemed to slam against her ribs. 'I shouldn't have assumed that you'd find me attractive enough to put yourself to any trouble for my sake.' She was horrified to hear the words pouring out, and utterly powerless to stop herself from saying them. 'I was just a little entertainment, wasn't I?'

He sat down on the log, a careful distance away. 'I don't know where to begin.'

'You don't have to explain.' She didn't want to hear an analysis of where she'd gone wrong; she simply wanted to be alone with her pain. But he obviously wasn't going anywhere, so the next best idea was to change the subject. 'What you're doing with the Works is a wonderful move, Dillon. You'll be glad you kept it.'

'I might not.' He shifted a little. 'Keep it, that is.'

Heidi was stunned. 'What?'

'I never said I wouldn't sell it, if the circumstances were right.'

'I know. But now that you're pouring money into it——'

'True. But it was worth almost nothing last month. Make it a viable concern again, and it's a whole different story.'

'Oh.' She felt blank. She supposed she should be glad if it came to that; seeing him around Fairview now and then—irregularly and without warning or a chance to prepare herself—would be agonizing, when she wanted so much more. Maybe it would be easier to know that all his ties were broken and he wouldn't be coming back at all. 'Well, of course. That's always an option, I suppose. I don't think you should count on a bid from Masters, though. I doubt he'd be interested in anything having to do with Fairview these days.'

Dillon seemed unsurprised; someone—Ken Ferris, no doubt—must have told him the outcome of Masters' proposal to the city council.

'I wouldn't sell it to him anyway,' he said deliberately. 'Any more than your father would a few years back.'

She blinked in astonishment. 'Masters wanted the Works then?'

'Oh, yes.'

'But I don't understand.'

Dillon sighed. He pulled up a stalk of grass from beside the log and began methodically cutting it into bits with his thumbnail. 'He was one of your father's bigger customers, but I never was sure why he wanted the Works. Maybe just because it wasn't for sale. But when Masters offered to buy it and your father said no, he started a behind-the-scenes campaign to take it over. And if he couldn't do that he'd destroy it and then pick up the pieces.'

Her throat was too tight to speak.

'I didn't know that then,' Dillon went on. 'I only knew it was suddenly easier to approach your father's customers, and I ended up with a good number of them. I was beating his prices, and servicing his accounts better—and I did the Works a great deal of damage, Heidi.'

'Normal business competition,' she said, almost under her breath.

'That's what it was. I swear to you there was nothing underhanded about it. It was altogether fair.' He added drily, 'Even Masters came to me to get his boxes for a while. I made him a very good deal.'

'Why?' Heidi was horrified.

'You must remember that I was completely unaware of why he was looking for another supplier. He only said he wasn't satisfied with the quality he was getting.'

She nodded. 'Of course.'

'He couldn't do without shipping boxes while he waited for the Works to drop into his hands, so he bought what he needed from me. I'm sure that once he had control of this plant he'd have promptly dropped me. Maybe he was hoping I'd miscalculate—count on his continued business and cut my profit margin too short— and he could hurt me while he was at it.'

'Why didn't you tell me this before, Dillon?'

He sighed. 'You'd made up your mind I was guilty— and the only conclusion I could reach was that your father had told you I'd been the villain rather than admit the truth and look like a fool.'

She shook her head. 'He didn't tell me. He was never one to share the details of his business, but I picked up pieces whenever I was home. I heard your name a lot, that last year. So when the pressure got bad, and then he sold the Works to you—and there wasn't enough money left to take care of everything...'

'You blamed me.'

She nodded. 'I couldn't add to his pain by demanding to know what had gone wrong. In any case, I thought I already knew.'

'That's understandable. But you see, when I thought he'd put the blame on me... Well, the only way I could explain was to make him look bad—and I didn't think you were likely to believe me.'

Heidi bit her lip. She wouldn't have believed him— then—and she was honest enough to admit it.

'I'm glad to know that's not what happened,' Dillon said simply. 'We'd always gotten along rather well personally, you see, and it hurt me to think that George would put the blame on me. Even though I'd been partly at fault, playing into Masters' hands by taking his customers——'

'That was why whenever the subject came up you felt guilty,' Heidi said. 'I could feel that you did, and it just made me more certain I was right.'

He nodded. 'But it wasn't me who moved in for the kill, Heidi. It wasn't until there was no other choice but to sell that your father called me and told me what was happening, and then I did what little I could to help.'

The statement was flat, unemotional. He'd bought a failing business, Heidi thought. A worthless one, one he didn't want, in an effort to make things better. And if it hadn't been for his help...

'I wouldn't base a business decision on a matter of physical pleasure', he'd said once. But to base it on friendship, on ethics, on doing what he felt was right... Yes, that made sense, now. Everything made sense, including the renovation of the Works, and also the black and bitter fury he had turned on her when she had blamed him for her father's death. Perhaps he had in a sense blamed himself for that as well.

His eyes were bleak. 'I'm not giving you a very flattering view of your father, am I? I've thought about it many times, and wondered why George didn't fight a little harder. Maybe he was already ill and had lost interest in the business. Or maybe his tame assistant had more control over things than was good for the Works.'

Tame assistant? Barry Evans, of course. No wonder Dillon's first move had been to get rid of him. 'It doesn't matter any more why it happened. I'm glad you told me.'

There didn't seem to be anything to say after that. They sat quietly on the log. Together, Heidi thought, and yet a million miles apart.

Finally, she said, 'So you bought the mortgage to give Mother some peace of mind. She was right, Dillon. You're—very sweet.'

'No,' he said. 'I'm not sweet, and that's not why I bought it.' He paused, and added, 'I was going to make you a wedding gift of it.'

His voice was as cool and unemotional as if he were reciting the multiplication tables. For a few seconds Heidi wasn't certain she'd heard him right, but then the words sank into her heart and she started to shiver. If that had been his intention . . .

But even if he had meant it once it didn't mean he felt the same way now. After the things she had believed of him, the things she had accused him of—without ever once asking for his side of the story . . .

No, he couldn't mean it any more. Still, the knowledge that once he had wanted to marry her was a precious gift, one she would hold close in her heart forever.

'I thank you for that,' she whispered. 'I'm sorry, Dillon. I'm so very sorry . . .'

She thought the silence would go on forever. Then the grass rustled as he stood up, and she braced herself for the awful loneliness that would descend when he walked away from her for the last time.

'Is that the end of it, then?' he said. His voice was almost gentle.

She started to tremble once more. 'Isn't it?'

'I don't know. You said a little while ago that once you'd assumed I found you attractive enough to put myself to some trouble for your sake.'

'I said I was silly to think that.'

'I don't agree. Would you like to know how much trouble I've put myself to, for your sake?'

'The mortgage, you mean? But——'

'That was the least of it. I think I told you once that I don't make business decisions for personal reasons?'

She nodded.

'Well, I lied.'

Heidi frowned. He wasn't making sense; they'd been over all this. 'You mean where my father was concerned? You don't need to explain that, or apologize for it.'

'No. I mean keeping the Works open. I came to Fairview to give my approval to close it down—it was almost a rhetorical question, the answer was so obvious. But then... I met you, and suddenly everything changed.'

She swallowed. The effort was painful.

'The moment we met we started striking sparks off each other, and I knew this was no ordinary relationship. This was the one I'd been looking for. And I thought you felt the same. The fire in you—the way you reacted to me even when you didn't want to... Was it my imagination, Heidi?'

Heidi remembered that first kiss, when she had practically turned to cinders in his arms, and shook her head. 'No,' she whispered. 'But I thought—I was afraid you weren't serious, that I was only a pastime, and that if I allowed myself to love you... I'd lose myself in the process. So I destroyed the very thing I wanted most.'

Dillon shook his head. 'You tried,' he said softly. 'And I tried to wipe out my feelings for you, too. When you told me you thought I'd killed your father——'

'You were so angry, I was terrified.'

'That was wise. I think I was dangerous, I was so angry. But even then I couldn't deny that I wanted you. That I loved you.'

Heidi would never know how she got into his arms— whether she jumped up from the log and flung herself at him, or whether he pulled her close. Not that it mattered; the only thing she needed to know was that this was where she belonged, where she would always belong—close to his heart.

There was a long space of time when there were no words; there was no need for any. Finally, though, Heidi buried her face in his shoulder and said indistinctly, 'Will it be all right? The Works, I mean.'

Dillon rubbed his cheek against her hair. 'Oh, yes. I won't say I didn't have to look awfully hard for a way to keep it operating at a profit. I am still a businessman, you know—not a philanthropist.'

Heidi peeked up at him. 'I'm not sure I'd agree with that,' she said doubtfully.

'And it took a while to convince my own advisers and my board of directors that revamping the Works and making it my base of operations was a good idea.'

'You mean—you're going to make it your head office?'

'Why not? I didn't think you'd want to leave Fairview, or Lilac Hill.'

She was utterly and breathlessly ecstatic. 'Dillon——' She paused. 'What about the bed-and-breakfast?'

'Run it if you like, give it up if you like.' He shrugged. 'Lilac Hill doesn't have to pay for itself any more.'

'And your idea of a corporate retreat?' Heidi said doubtfully.

'I think I threw that at you mainly to keep you from wondering why I'd bothered with the mortgage. I was so furious with you right then, and with myself for being stupid enough to believe you might care about me enough to forgive the past, that I think I'd have said anything to hurt you.'

She stroked his cheek tenderly. 'I cared enough. I felt like a fool to deny what my head said was true—but I cared.'

'Funny way you had of showing it. Of course I have to entertain my customers sometimes, and I'd like to do that at Lilac Hill. But if it's all right with you I'd like to keep it mainly as a retreat for us, and our friends. And our family, someday.' His voice was husky. 'That reminds me. I'd better talk to your mother about buying the rest of the house from her. Not that she won't be welcome to live with us, but just in case she wants the option...'

Heidi pulled his head down to kiss him again, and it was a good deal later before Dillon said unsteadily, 'I'm sorry I couldn't tell you what I had in mind for the Works. I couldn't talk to anybody, you see, until I knew it would work. There was too much danger of a leak. And I especially couldn't talk to you——'

'When I was championing Masters as the savior of the Works?' Her tone was wry. 'I can see why you'd hesitate.'

'I did talk to the mayor, though, and filled him in on what George had told me.'

'I thought you were pleading for concessions for yourself.'

There was a smile in his voice. 'Only where you're concerned, Heidi.' He kissed her again and added thoughtfully, 'I'll have to join the Ambassadors, I suppose. If I'm going to be in business in this town...'

She smiled up at him, her heart too full to tell him how happy she was.

'Do you mind?'

Heidi brushed her hands across his shoulders as if measuring their breadth, and whispered, 'Mind? Heavens, no. I'll order your green coat tomorrow.'

EPILOGUE

Two years later

LILAC HILL
Dillon and Heidi Archer

2 a.m.

Dear Heidi,

I can't sleep, and you looked so comfortable—and so exhausted—that I couldn't bear to disturb you to tell you what I'm thinking. So I'll leave this note on your dressing-table where you'll find it in the morning.

I can't thank you enough for making room in your life for the other woman in mine. For not feeling threatened by how important she is to me. For teaching me that love isn't divided when there are two objects of it, but multiplied instead. For sharing all the...

But I see she's waking up, and any moment now she'll let out a bellow that will carry all the way down the hall and wake you, even though I've got the baby monitor right here. So I'd better stop this letter and give our daughter her middle-of-the-night bottle.

Thank you for the most precious gift I've ever received—the other woman in my life. I love you, darling.

Dillon

HARLEQUIN SUPERROMANCE®

WOMEN WHO DARE
They take chances, make changes
and follow their hearts!

FORBIDDEN
by Ellen James

Having proposed marriage and been turned down flat,
Dana Morgan says to hell with security, her ex-lover and
her old life. Out for adventure, she's prepared for difficulties
and discomfort—and she's eagerly looking forward to the
unpredictable.

What she isn't prepared for is Nick Petrie. Talk about *unpredictable*... And Nick knows it; in fact, he enjoys his reputation.
While Dana tells him to his face that he's a "royal pain," pri-
vately she has to admit he's the handsomest, sexiest, most
exciting man she's ever met. Unfortunately, Nick swears
there's no room in his life for love.

Dana's taking the chance that he's wrong.

Watch for *Forbidden* by Ellen James.
Available in April 1995,
wherever Harlequin books are sold.

HARLEQUIN ROMANCE®

brings you

When you read **Invitation to Love** by Leigh Michaels,
you will know there are some wonderful reading hours
ahead of you with our **SEALED WITH A KISS** titles!

In April we have chosen **Dearest Love**, by Betty Neels,
Harlequin Romance #3355, all about sensible
Arabelle Lorimer and the rich and handsome
Dr. Titus Tavener, who both seem to be agreed on
one thing—that they make a very suitable couple.
But what happens when love unexpectedly
enters the picture?

Look out for the next two titles:

Harlequin Romance #3361
Mail Order Bridegroom
by Day Leclaire in May

Harlequin Romance #3366
P.S. I Love You
by Valerie Parv in June

SWAK-2R

Available wherever Harlequin books are sold

HARLEQUIN SUPERROMANCE®

**He's sexy, he's single...and he's a father!
Can any woman resist?**

First Love, Second Chance
By Amanda Clark

Julia Marshall is leaving New York City and going back to the
Pennsylvania town where she grew up—even if there's not
much to go back for. She'd been raised by cold, unloving foster
parents. And she'd been betrayed by *Tommy Black,* the love of
her teenage years. He'd promised to wait for her, to marry her,
to love her forever. And he hadn't....

Now, ten years later, Tommy's a family man—with a family of
two, consisting of him and his five-year-old daughter, Charlotte,
better known as Chipper. When Julia comes back to town,
Tommy discovers that he'd like nothing better than to make
that a family of three....

Watch for *First Love, Second Chance* in April.
Available wherever Harlequin books are sold.

If you are looking for more titles by

LEIGH MICHAELS

Don't miss these fabulous stories by one of
Harlequin's most renowned authors:

Harlequin Romance®

#03184	OLD SCHOOL TIES	$2.89	☐
#03214	THE BEST-MADE PLANS	$2.89	☐
#03233	THE UNEXPECTED LANDLORD	$2.89	☐
#03248	SAFE IN MY HEART	$2.89	☐
#03263	TIES THAT BLIND	$2.89	☐
#03275	THE LAKE EFFECT	$2.99	☐
#03300	A SINGULAR HONEYMOON	$2.99	☐
#03337	THE ONLY SOLUTION	$2.99 U.S.	☐
		$3.50 CAN.	

(limited quantities available on certain titles)

TOTAL AMOUNT	$	
POSTAGE & HANDLING	$	
($1.00 for one book, 50¢ for each additional)		
APPLICABLE TAXES*	$	
TOTAL PAYABLE	$	

(check or money order—please do not send cash)

To order, complete this form and send it, along with a check or money order
for the total above, payable to Harlequin Books, to: **In the U.S.:** 3010 Walden
Avenue, P.O. Box 9047, Buffalo, NY 14269-9047; **In Canada:** P.O. Box 613,
Fort Erie, Ontario, L2A 5X3.

Name: _____

Address: _____ City: _____

State/Prov.: _____ Zip/Postal Code: _____

*New York residents remit applicable sales taxes.
 Canadian residents remit applicable GST and provincial taxes.   HLMBACK2

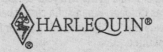

♦HARLEQUIN®